Miss Jackson

Acknowledgements

I would like to thank all those who have helped with the production of this book and given me the encouragement to put pen to paper. In particular I would like to thank my friend Dr David Arthey and also my niece Helen Jackson for the wonderful drawings on pages 43, 81 and 137 (drawn at the age of five years nine months).

Ruth Jackson

Front cover – Ruth Jackson on her mother's knee with brother Oliver standing to the right.

Rear cover – Ruth on the left, Oliver at the rear and baby Joyce on the right.

Little
Miss Jackson

by

Eleanor Ruth
Jackson

Bolero

First Published by Bolero Books 2003

ISBN: 0-9538452-3-0

A catalogue record for this book is available from the British Library.

Bolero Books is an imprint of Plum Tree Publishing Limited, Worcester, England, WR7 4NX

Printed and bound in Great Britain

Contents

Introduction

Whatever your views on the relative importance of heredity and environment in the development of a child, you probably agree that each is of some importance, so without apology I start by telling you something of my parents' pedigrees.

My mother, Eleanor Bomford, came from a long line of Worcestershire farmers whose lineage can be traced back to the sixteenth century, staunch supporters of Protestant beliefs. Cromwell once took breakfast with them at Wyre Piddle and two Bomfords fought for him at the battle of Worcester. Later, another was awarded a large estate in Ireland. By the nineteenth century the family had spread widely across the county.

One blazing hot August day in 1875, when George Frederick Bomford was pitching sheaves up on to a rick at The Common, Atch Lench, a messenger came running to tell him that the baby his wife was expecting had arrived, another girl, the fifth girl and no boy yet. He was bitterly disappointed for what farmer could afford to give so many girls good educations, and possibly dowries, when there was no son to help with farm work and to carry on the family name. The child born on that hot summer day was named Eleanor and in due course became my mother.

My father's family history is totally different. John Jackson appeared in Berkshire at about the same time as the Kennet-Avon Canal and he may have been a navvy. He got a girl into trouble, had to marry her and seems to have helped his father-in-law with his work, believed to have been the making of tallow candles. John's family was extremely poor and there was more than one pauper funeral, but his youngest son moved into Reading and ran a chandler's business mentioned in directories of the town. In his lifetime his family seems to have become Baptist and his grandsons all did well. In 1875, his grandson Edward married and the couple lived over their small shop. At that period enterprise and hard work paid, the business developed rapidly and today Jackson's Corner is one of the best thought-of shops in Reading.

Edward had three sons and by the time their youngest, Arnold Frank, was born, in 1883, they no longer lived over the shop and the children could be well-educated.

One summer evening in 1895, the three Jackson boys went down town to hear the result of the General Election declared. Rufus Isaacs won a place in Parliament and great was the jubilation of the young Liberals, who chanted "RU-fus-I-saacs-RU-fus-I-saacs".... Then they took the horses out of the shafts of the new M.P.'s carriage and set out to push and pull the new M.P. home. As may be imagined, the supporters gradually melted away and the Jackson boys began to wonder if there would be enough manpower left to get up the last hill but, with some difficulty, this was achieved. The stars shone down, as the boys, tired and happy and mightily pleased with themselves, got home. I wonder if, when Sir Rufus became Viceroy of India and Lord Reading, he ever thought of that triumphal ride?

At the age of sixteen, it was time for Arnold to decide how he would earn his living. Both elder brothers were already in the business, which was not yet large enough to warrant taking in a third son. Looking over a hedge at a pretty scene with a herd of cows grazing contentedly in a field ablaze with buttercups in bright sunshine, he told his father he thought he would like to be a farmer. So they set about making him into a farmer and he was soon placed as a farming pupil with a good Baptist family who successfully farmed many acres on the Worcestershire - Warwickshire border.

Meanwhile Eleanor, the middle child in a family of nine, was educated at a school successfully run by two aunts with assistants, and which was a very short distance from her home. In due course Fred and other younger siblings went there too. Here some explanation seems necessary. The aunts ran a school mainly for girls but took boys in the lower forms, as did many other girls' schools, a custom which continued right up to the Second World War and perhaps afterwards. (I taught in such a school from 1936-1938.)

In Fred's case the school, run by his aunts, was just down the village street from his home. The village school was about a mile distant and was a Church of England school. The family had a long Baptist tradition, was very well read and spoke grammatically. Also there was a class difference between children of employer and employees. The nearest boys' school was probably five miles away and not geared to teaching small children. So at the age of four or so Fred attended the school run by his aunts and later moved to a boys' school. There were no school buses.

All the children of this family were born Liberals except Fred who was two years younger than my mother. He was a Conservative from birth. Once before a General Election a Liberal poster was put on a barn wall facing the village street. Every morning on his way to school Fred stopped and threw mud at it. Eleanor, carrying a wet sponge, made a point of following him and cleaning the poster before continuing on her way!

Eventually Eleanor passed the equivalent of three A-levels, (English, History, Scripture and a compulsory Arithmetic paper) sitting the examination at Cheltenham Ladies' College. This qualified her to teach in a select girls' boarding school, where she stayed only one year, as she was not particularly happy there. For a time she was governess to a young relation and then kept house for her brother Fred, who was already farming but not yet married.

Big families of reasonably well-educated young people found all sorts of things to do together. Among other activities there was tennis, cycling, croquet, mixed hockey and paper-chases which necessitated young men helping their lady partners over difficult stiles and carrying them across brooks. So it is not to be wondered at that Arnold and Eleanor soon met.

After several years as a farming pupil, Arnold spent nearly a year working in Scotland at Edzell, a wild rough life, where he had to learn a new language to understand the men. Then, after two terms at Reading College of Agriculture, he was considered ready to farm on his own and, no doubt with financial help from his father, rented Glenmore Farm at Wick and married Eleanor in September 1906. Their son Oliver was born two years later.

On Lady Day 1910 they left Wick and became tenants of Ford Hill Farm on the Cotswolds. Here they enjoyed the clear fresh air, the wide open views, the splendid spectacle of Halle's Comet in the night sky and on summer evenings children from the farm cottages playing age-old singing games near the house. An idyllic life, though they worked very hard. Here I was conceived and here born….and thereby hangs a tale.

Sunday 31st of December 1911 was a beautiful sunny day and in the afternoon my father harnessed his beloved nag Daisy to the trap and he and my mother proposed to go for a drive. To this the monthly nurse agreed if she went with them. Soon my mother decided that they should turn homewards and then preparations were made for my arrival. To fetch Dr. Alexander, Dad cycled down to Broadway. It was a gated road. I think there were three gates on the farm drive and six or seven on the public road. In due course the doctor arrived in his gig. Before midnight I arrived too and hopefully became…

"The child that is born on the Sabbath Day
Is bonny and blithe and good and gay!"

On Tuesday the second of January snow came, deep snow, which was cleared from the roads by men with shovels, snow that lay on the roadsides till April.

1.

THE FIRST TEN YEARS

O the days gone by!
The apples in the orchard, and the pathway through the rye;
When the bloom was on the clover, and blue was in the sky,

The childish faith in fairies, and Aladdin's magic ring –
The simple, soul-reposing, glad belief in everything –
When life was like a story holding neither sob nor sigh,
In the golden, olden glory of the days gone by.

Selected lines from J.W. Riley.

Of my early days at Ford Hill, I remember nothing. By Michaelmas 1913, Dad was ready to buy a farm, so we came down from the hills to Thorn, where he had bought one farm and rented the adjoining one.

Oliver and I went with our mother to stay at her old home, while stock was driven or transported more than twenty miles on a high-sided dray and machinery was brought on farm wagons, all horse-drawn. I think the furniture may have been moved professionally. Kathleen, a teenage girl from one of the cottages, came for some weeks to help us settle into our new home, which, being medieval, was much more difficult to manage than Ford.

The difficulties that were noticed immediately were the rough stone floors in all but one of the ground floor rooms. Drinking water had to be carried from a pump some distance from the back door, rainwater from a tank in another direction. Firewood was stored in a shed near the pump, coal was kept even further from the house.

My first memory is of toddling behind Kathleen as she went, at dusk, to bring logs from the woodshed for the open fire... but it was not long before I was playing alone on the lawn at dusk and saw the great green eyes of a wild farm cat. A year or two later, it was I who discovered a patch of winter aconites. By the time I saw a red squirrel, I was old enough to describe it and be told what it was. I have never seen another in this district.

Though very attached to Oliver, I find it is the things I did alone, discovered for myself, that I remember most vividly. How fortunate I was, always to have had so much space, so much fresh air, so much freedom.

The time soon came for Oliver to have more schooling than our mother had time to give, so a governess was found. She was the daughter of the local stone mason and, not long before, had been a pupil at a boarding school. So Miss Cox came into our lives and was immediately christened "Cockie". What a wonderful person she was! Our daily routine was something like this – Family breakfast at 8 a.m. in the nursery, where, in winter, there was a good wood fire in the grate and of course a solid guard in front of it – Lessons from 9.30 to 11.00 then half an hour break with snacks called "lunch". More school work from 11.30 to 12.30 and that was that! With individual attention the length of time for study was adequate and as Cockie was often "living in" she was available to amuse and teach us lots of useful and entertaining things.

I believe that at this period most farmers paid their men when they finished work at midday on Saturday, but at Thorn it was done after work on Friday, the arrangement being made so that wives could shop on Saturday morning. When Dad went out, carrying cash box and book, I usually went with him. He settled himself on a chair at the far end of the back kitchen table, in winter lit a candle, and laid out all that he needed. Meanwhile I settled myself at the other end of the table and the men were all leaning on the courtyard wall. They came in one by one in order of seniority, carter first and youngest ploughboy last. When the business was finished, I was given 1d. (one old penny), my "wages for the week".

In all my life I have seen only one Shepherd's Ark and it stood in our rickyard. It had been brought down from the Cotswolds, where it would have been more at home, out on the wolds at lambing time. It stood on four large iron wheels, had shafts at one end and, at the other, a door and a small window. Strong wooden steps could be hooked below the doorway. This made a wonderful house for children's play and many happy hours we and young visitors spent there. It gradually became furnished in a haphazard sort of way with blocks of wood, cracked and chipped crockery, pictures on the walls. Sometimes in summer we even slept there.

Years later, when a plum orchard had been planted and was bearing fruit, the Ark was taken there to act as an office and as shelter for fruit weighed up in chip baskets and waiting over night to be taken to Evesham market in the early morning. Later, when the "bottom fell out of the plum market", the orchard was grubbed up and the Ark was left standing there and became a sort of annex to a nearby caravan, which housed one lonely man.

I am sorry that there is no photograph, especially as, when, a generation later my brother Oliver retired, the ark was found to be in too bad a condition to be moved to the local history museum.

Easter holidays brought the first picnics of the year. On Good Fridays, which always seemed to be bright and sunny, we, the whole family and any visitors, made our way to Atch Lench, where we met one or more families of cousins and set out walking to "The Wood" carrying everything we needed for a successful picnic. We found carpets of primroses, patches of violets, anemones, cowslips, a few false oxlips, early purple orchis and an occasional herb Paris. Those with sharper eyes than mine found birds' nests and, if Easter was not too early, we hoped to hear the cuckoo.

An uncle, aunt and cousin usually came to stay with us at this time of year. We all went on a picnic to "The Long Meadow" (now a nature-reserve). Those who wished could travel on a horse drawn dray, for fencing poles, cut during the winter, were to be collected and taken home. A fire was lit, tea made and white and blue violets and cowslips were found in abundance. It was too early, however, to hope to find a green-veined orchis. A jolly occasion for all!

While this family was with us, we all went to the Mill House, where the farm weighing machine was kept. There we were all weighed in stones and pounds. And a record was kept, written in pencil on an inside door, and there it remained until the farm was sold.

Later in the year there were teas in the hay and harvest fields. When the men were working late, they were provided with sustenance, which had to be delivered to rick and field. So two large cans of tea and two large packets of jam sandwiches had to be delivered to the rick, where one lot was left and the other travelled to the field in an empty wagon, Sometimes we took our tea and if Dad was working there, he joined us.

Many many years later, on a glorious summer day my parents and I were having tea indoors but could hear wagons moving and men shouting at the Dutch Barn. This was the first year Dad had been too old to work alongside them. Suddenly he said, "And to think they're pitching sheaves and I'm not there." The most poignant moment of my life!

So many of the things I recount of this period cannot be dated. They happened again and again, but in 1915 we went on a family holiday, I suppose money was a little more available than in former years, for farming tends to do well in wartime. I was taken completely by surprise. I had no idea that anything was planned. We travelled by train to Newquay in Cornwall and I well remember my first sight of the sea. I loved the beach but was frightened of the big waves and thought of the sea as some enormous bath, the temperature of which could be controlled, and called out for the hot tap to be turned on, for I had met hot taps at my grandfather's house at Reading. When my plea failed

I called out that Mother hadn't put enough clothes on me! I was teased about this for many years. Later I was sorry about being afraid of the water, for Dad was a strong swimmer, but with strokes that would now be called old-fashioned. He swam with Oliver on his back. As was common at that period, we had rented rooms, two bedrooms and a sitting room. Each day my mother shopped for food and the landlady cooked and served it. One day I saw an army officer go into a shop and come out with a black band round his arm. I asked about this and the answer I received gave me my first understanding of war. Cockie had gone with us and some relations from Reading were there at the same time, so Cockie looked after all the children in the afternoons, while the others rested or walked or enjoyed outings.

One bright May morning in 1916, Oliver and I were playing in the court, when gypsies came to the back door selling pegs. On seeing us, they asked my mother if the Master would like to buy a donkey for the children and she told them to bring the donkey in the evening and he would look at it. At one o'clock dinner, Dad was told and didn't definitely say "no"! In the evening Oliver and I started up the drive and the poplar trees were silhouetted against a gloriously red sky. Then we saw a man and a boy, with a pony and a donkey, trotting through the gateway. I was lifted onto the donkey and Oliver onto the pony and we were steadied by brown hands as we rode home. Dad came out and examined the mouth of a light grey donkey, with no cross on her back. Apparently this needs explanation, so I have done some research. True asses, sometimes called "Jerusalem donkeys" are native to north east Africa and this donkey conformed in most respects. Her short hair was pale grey, her ears large, her tail not very hairy, however a true ass should have a dark mane, the colour continuing down the length of the spine. Across the shoulders is another stripe of dark hair, so forming a cross. There are of course other breeds of donkeys and ancestry is often very mixed.

In my young days most grown-ups and children expected to see a cross on a donkey's back and many knew the legend concerning its origin, for it was believed that the cross had been given as a reward for the part played by a donkey on the first Palm Sunday and to remind people that donkeys should be treated with kindness and respect.

After this digression I must add that the donkey

had a full mouth and that the gypsies whipped her mercilessly as they put her through her paces. A bargain was struck and "Jane" became one of the family!

The local saddler made a riding bridle to measure. A second-hand donkey cart and set of rather battered harness was bought from a farmer whose children had long outgrown interest in their own ancient donkey.

The young Jacksons with Cockie in the donkey cart became a familiar sight in the neighbourhood and when Cockie was selling flags for the Red Cross, cart and harness were decorated with flags and, as we drove around, I imagine we did a roaring trade.

On Sunday afternoons, Dad usually walked to see stock in outlying fields and Oliver and I went with him, taking turns to ride Jane who often came too. So one Sunday in the Autumn of 1917 we were inspecting a herd of young cattle in The Long Meadow. These cattle had never before seen a donkey, let alone a little girl riding one and, as we turned to come home, they chased Jane. Jane galloped. Eventually I fell off. Dad picked me up and carried me, a fattish five-year-old, all the way home, Oliver caught and led Jane. I was hurt and frightened as I could not bend my right elbow. The doctor was sent for, but the joint set wrongly and it gave trouble for a long time. Even today I think I could be identified by an X-ray of that elbow!

By the time of this accident our family life was changing. Oliver was old enough for a real school and attended a day school in Evesham and stayed Monday to Friday with cousins. Ronald, the son of a neighbouring farmer, joined me for lessons. He was my first school friend. I was always Daddy's girl and whenever I could, went with him as he drove out in the trap, drawn by our dear nag Daisy. So Friday afternoons, I went to Evesham. Daisy was stabled at The Railway Hotel, while we went to the bank to get money to pay the men and then did other farm business. How cold those drives could be, though I was well wrapped up and over my knees had a mackintosh rug with a warm lining. There was a great welcome for Oliver and hot buttered toast for tea!

In June 1917 an aunt from Reading came to stay and when she went home, I went with her. Knowing Grandpa J and his house and garden from previous visits, I was delighted. Every morning after breakfast, Grandpa went down town to business, Mr Love the "coachman" driving him in a "tub" drawn by a smart high-stepping pony. Very often I went too. If Mr

Love had been given jobs to do in town, I stayed with Grandpa in his office, which had "Counting House" printed on the door. He always found things to amuse me. One day the pony had to be taken to be shod and I went with Mr Love. I had seen many horses shod, one after another at the village forge, but on this particular day the army had brought a group of mules and there were several smiths at work at the same time. There were mules kicking and soldiers swearing. What an exciting time!

The sun seemed to shine every day. Later in the morning I sat on the veranda doing simple sums and writing wise sayings in a copy book and embroidering a bulldog standing on a Union Jack – remember there was a war on! It was worked in tent stitch on printed canvas, but I did only the easy parts. Afterwards it was made into a teapot holder for me to give my mother, I have it still. At 11a.m. a maid came with glasses of hot milk for all who were at home.

On Saturday mornings, the gardener brought flowers to the house and my aunt and I went down to King's Road Chapel, where she "did the flowers". I don't know if anyone else ever took a turn. So, on Sunday mornings we saw the flowers again, for we went to morning service.

There were toys galore that had belonged to a previous generation. How I loved the Noah's Ark. Once Aunt E. lent me a mandolin she had had as a girl, but of course I couldn't play it and no more could she!

Never being afraid to be alone, I was often left to my own devices and I had the run of the big gardens, the wood, the green houses and stable yard and no doubt often hindered the men who were working there. Only once was I homesick and that was when I looked down at the smooth green grass and for a moment thought I was on the lawn at home.

So June slipped away and one morning Aunt E. received a letter and told me that I had a baby sister. My immediate reply was, "I hope she'll wear spect-acles like me!" but to myself I said, "I shan't let it make any difference to the way I go on!"

With Cockie away nursing her own mother and inadequate help in the farmhouse, an S.O.S. was sent by telegram and within 24 hours my mother, baby Joyce and Oliver joined us in Reading. Joyce now 23 days old had slept all the way. Then one Saturday, without warning, Dad turned up in time for dinner, having left all animals in charge of stockmen. What a joy to have all the family together and to be living in the lap of luxury!

That afternoon Dad took Oliver and me and an older cousin on the river and tried to teach us how to row. Later he reported that Oliver got on fairly well but that I was hopeless! Please! I was only five and had never before seen a rowing boat! What a wonderful day! Alas, Dad went home again on Sunday afternoon and eventually the day came for us all to go home. We went down to the station and waited on the long platform. Our train was late, very late. At last a long train pulled up, but it was not ours. The front coaches had been adapted to have four bunks in each compartment and under a grey blanket on each bunk lay a completely motionless man. Red Cross nurses flitted about. At the back of the train there were cheerful soldiers with comparatively minor injuries, arms in slings or limping on crutches. They were laughing and joking, glad to be back in England with a "blighty"!* People around us were saying the train was going down to the West Country and it was the first time I heard that expression. Whenever I stand on that platform I still see the ghost of that train. (This was in early August 1917 and students of the First World War will know where these soldiers had been fighting.)

Home sweet home and I was still Daddy's girl, though in many ways I must have been a disappointment to him. He was so fond of animals and cared for them in sickness and in health, whereas I, perhaps like many another child, soon lost interest in pets. Someone gave me bantams, a cock and a few hens and a little house to keep them in. For a time it was fun looking after them, feeding them, collecting and eating their eggs, shutting them up at night and so on, but I really was not very sorry when a fox got into their shed and killed the lot. I never looked after a pet rabbit properly, but, looking back, I think it was a great mistake for someone to have given me a rabbit in such a small hutch. I bottle fed a pet lamb fairly well, but when he was nearly ready to join the flock in the field, he must have eaten something poisonous and died. He had a grand funeral and a gravestone!

Horses I always loved, though of course I never had to groom them! When I was quite young, perhaps five, Oliver and I went for a walk and, finding two young shire horses with heads hanging over a gate towards us, stopped to stroke them. The name of one

**A "blighty one" – A wound ensuring repatriation from the front.*

was Merryman, but the farm men called him Snapper. We were wearing little white linen hats and Snapper suddenly snatched Oliver's from his head and chewed it up. Finding it not particularly to his liking, he spat it out all green and slimy. So we picked it up and carried it home. There was no trouble and after the next washing day it was as good as new!

To be shod, a horse was led to the blacksmiths, about a mile along a road which is fairly busy nowadays, but then there was rarely any traffic, sometimes no traffic at all. There might be a short queue of horses at the forge and a plough boy could make this last all the afternoon. So I was soon allowed to lead the more staid horses and enjoyed my job for which I was paid one penny when I got home. To this day there are people in the village who recall their parents being appalled that one so small was allowed to lead such large horses!

Time passed, the war was over, but I was still having lessons in the morning only. It was haymaking time and in the afternoons I enjoyed myself leading a horse drawing a wagon on to which two men tossed hay and another loaded it safely. I don't suppose I was really much help, for the horse would probably have moved forward or stopped at a shout from the men, but I held the rein. Then came from behind us an airship, very low, very noisy. Neither men, nor horse, nor I had ever seen or heard an airship before. The horse tossed its head and leapt forward and I was lifted high above the ground. The airship sailed away. A little later Dad arrived to see that all was well and I heard the carter say, " 'Er never let go". Since then I have realised what a mercy that was, as, had I let go, I should have been under the wheels of the wagon.

A job by which I could supplement my pocket money of 1d. a week was potatoing. In the autumn the fields were ready for "harvesting" and for this extra work, casual labour was employed. A horse drawn machine, called a spinner, dug one row of "spuds" at a time and flung them out on to open ground. The row was divided into equal lengths marked out by tall poles and each length had two "pickers-up", mostly women. Near the row, the machine left a mound of earth with some potatoes showing, but it was necessary to scuffle about with feet to find any that were hidden. There were other potatoes flung about irregularly on the surface of the ground and further from the row. I suppose I was about six when I first went to “help” Dad and we worked together, I doing the easy work gathering surface potatoes and we had a short pitch as from time to time he had to go to help any workers who were getting behind and slowing down the whole process. Lessons in the morning and three hours potatoing in the afternoon – all most enjoyable and three pence earned (old pence). To complete the picture, workers put the potatoes in buckets and then tipped them into round hampers called “skips”. A horse and cart came along the row and with them came a man who emptied the skips into the cart which went to the bury where they were emptied. The potatoes were then covered with straw and “earthed up” to protect them from winter frosts.

As I grew older my pay rose and after some years I remember Dad saying I was now worth a woman’s wage of five old pence an hour.... And I remember another afternoon... as we finished work, it was cold and slightly misty and the sun, a red ball of fire, was low in the sky. It was a glorious sight and I said to myself, “The very gate of Heaven.”

I continued to enjoy potatoing and when I went to school it often coincided with half-term. Even when I was teaching it was often one of my half-term ploys.

Of course there were other ways of supplementing pocket money. Oliver and I had been scrap metal merchants from our early days. As soon as we were able to roam about ploughed fields, we picked up old horse shoes and ploughshares and made a heap of old iron near our home. When Dad thought we had a sufficient quantity we contacted the local blacksmith who came with a horse and trap, made an offer and took our hoard away. On one occasion he paid us as much as ten shillings.

When I was at school, the summer term did not end until late July and we went back again in late September... In those days farm hedge cropping was done by hand and some were left to grow for many years and grow tall so that they could be laid. These conditions made it possible to pick and market blackberries, so I arranged with the local carrier to bring chip baskets from Evesham. The following Monday morning they were full and weighed and carried to the top of our drive in time for him to take them by horse and cart to Evesham market. Some days later I received a meagre postal order for the sale of the fruit less the auctioneer's commission... and there was still the carrier to pay.

1918 was the year of the cuckoo! Never before or since have I heard such a cuckooing! For some hours every day, Joyce sat in her pram in the garden and soon was answering them in their own language and cuckoo was the first word she said.

One sunny summer morning she was put with her playthings on a mackintosh rug with a wide area of lawn round it. Though not able to walk she was fairly mobile. From time to time our mother looked from the kitchen window to see that she was all right. Then came the time when Joyce was not there and nowhere to be seen. We went out to look for her. There was no hiding place nearby. From lawn to rickyard a wide path had been scythed through long grass and we followed this hopefully. Then what did we see? Joyce sitting beside the grindstone and at her other side sat a fox cub but, seeing us, the cub trotted gently away. I still see all this vividly but J. has no memory of it at all.

In 1919, with the war over, it was time for parents to take their noses off the grindstone occasionally. Early in that year or the next Oliver and I were taken to a pantomime in Birmingham and it was a complete eye-opener to me. Some scenes fixed themselves indelibly on my mind. At home we built houses of playing cards, but here there were card houses big enough for real people to run in and out. Joyce had been left at home with a young maid.

In the summer we had another seaside holiday, this time at Llandudno. Again Joyce was left at home and this time one of my mother's sisters brought her little girl and looked after the house and any necessary farm duties. We travelled by train from Alcester station, via Birmingham, Crewe and Chester... But how did we get the seven miles to Alcester? Of course we went by horse and trap, parents in front, children behind facing backwards, luggage under seat.

It was a hot summer morning and all went well until we were approaching Alcester and then Daisy, the mare, slipped and fell on a patch of melted tar on the road. Front seat passengers were thrown out. Back seat passengers were safe. Parents picked themselves up. Daisy was helped to her feet, knees not broken, shaft not broken, no clothes torn or spattered with tar! Master and horse comforted each other, and the journey continued.

But how did the horse and trap get home? A farm worker came to the station by bicycle, which he strapped on the back of the trap, and then drove gently home.

1921 was the year of the eel! The summer was very hot and dry and there was scarcely any water in the brook, so Dad decided to have the stream cleaned out and it was soon discovered that there were lots of eels in it. The work was done by men with shovels, nothing mechanical about it. Every day, hoping to be working on the brook, each man brought a bucket with him and hoped to be able to carry home enough eels to give his family a really good meal. Looking back it seems that we ate fried eels for breakfast every day. I remember Dad skinning them and cutting them into chunks and how the chunks jumped about in the pan as Mother cooked them. It was always said that eels were full of electricity. Can it be true?

This year was notable in other ways. In Spring, Girl Guides came to the village and a whole new world opened up to me and I was connected with the movement for more than forty years, as brownie, guide, ranger, cadet, lieutenant, captain and district captain. At the end of December I had my tenth birthday and Brown Owl and all the Fairies and Elves came in uniform to my party.

Meanwhile our education had not been neglected. Oliver had gone to school in Evesham then to Reading School, first as day boy, then as boarder, but a few years later he was to come home and finish his schooling at Alcester Grammar School. Cockie's family had left the district, and she with them. Now Ronald, with whom I had shared lessons for years, and I went to a farmhouse about half way between our homes. Here there were two sisters, younger than us and all four of us shared a new governess known as Huntie. I, who had been taught to read from a book called "Reading without Tears", a book used by my mother and her siblings, was absolutely amazed by the "modern" books the young girls had!

Nor was religious education neglected. Our mother taught each of us bedside prayers and told us Bible stories from Old and New Testaments. After breakfast on Sundays we were installed in the Nursery. Our mother opened up used foolscap envelopes, which provided excellent paper for art work. On each she printed a text in large block letters and surrounded it with nature drawings, usually of flowers in season, and then we settled down to paint them.

Both parents were members of a small Baptist Church in a hamlet about five miles away. My memory is that we were taken there every Sunday morning, but my mother's diary shows there were many times when one of us was poorly, or roads were too icy for safe travel, or the "perfidious cowman" had not turned up and Dad had to stay at home to milk and look after stock. As babies, each of us in turn was put to sleep in a drawer from the kitchen dresser and placed under the back seat of the trap. The next stage of travelling was to sit in front between parents and by the time I was too big for this, and must sit at the back, Oliver was old enough to ride his bicycle. I remember times when two mackintosh rugs were in use and my Mother held a gig umbrella over the whole party. We had to start in good time as the horse had to be stabled before the service.

Every week there was a talk for children, but for several years we had a Minister from Wales and his speech was so different from ours that I never understood a word he said!

Though unable to attend Sunday School, we were invited to the "Treat" and usually managed to get there. Once when the governess was driving Jane, the "old moke" was so tired on the return journey that, from then on, she absolutely refused to set foot in that direction!

Sunday afternoons we usually spent with Dad as he walked round the fields counting and checking the health of flocks and herds as necessary… and there were hens to feed and eggs to be collected.

On Sundays in winter we had tea in the drawing room, where there was a piano, which Dad played and we learnt hymns. Our first carol was "Once in Royal David's City", one which I love to this day. Before meals we said Grace and the usual one was:

"God bless the food which now we take
To do us good for Jesus' sake.
Amen"

But on Sundays in summer we often had tea in the garden and sang:

"Let us with a gladsome mind
Praise the Lord, for he is kind:
For his mercies aye endure,
Ever faithful, ever sure."

Someone has asked what my mother did while the governess taught us. This I cannot answer but it behoves me to record something of the life of a farmer's wife in the early part of the twentieth century. I am appalled at the hard physical work she did and how little I helped her when I was old enough to have done so.

Firstly, I think about the medieval house and lack of indoor help, though I think that Cockie must often have stayed to lend a hand. There was no mains water or electricity. All water had to be carried from an outside pump or rainwater tank. Heating and lighting was provided by a coal-fired kitchen range, open fires, oil lamps, candles and a hurricane lantern outside. There was no maid living in until about the time that Joyce was born. There were no laundries or dry cleaners in the district.

Every day the kitchen range had to be 'done' and the fire laid and lit, kettles of water put on to heat and coal to be brought in, but I think Dad usually did this before he went to his farm duties. In winter, there were two other grates in use.

Three solid meals a day were served. Morning and evening the cowman brought buckets of milk to the house. This had to be strained and all equipment washed and scalded. Cream was skimmed from yesterday's milk and twice a week made into butter using a glass churn worked by hand... more scalding of equipment!

The bedrooms had carafes of drinking water for teeth, jugs of rainwater for washing and, of course, there were chamber pots! All liquid had to be carried upstairs and downstairs!

Monday was washing day and 'Reevsie,' a washerwoman, came and took charge of the back-kitchen, but I think that during the week, Dad had filled the furnace with rainwater and brought in coal for heating it. Early on Monday he lit the fire, so that Reevsie need waste no time. She dealt with clothes, bed linen, table linen (white, starched), towels used by the family and workers who came to the outside pump to wash.... Wet things were passed through a mangle and, if fine, were carried in clothes baskets and hung on washing lines on the 'drying green.' If wet, as much as possible was hung on clothes horses. Reevsie had a solid meal, stayed to finish work afterwards and then trudged one and a half miles home. In later years she lived in one of our farm cottages.

If washing had dried sufficiently, Tuesday was ironing day. The work was done by my Mother in the back-kitchen with four flat irons heated on the sides of an ironing stove (now in the Almonry Museum at Evesham). Then everything had to be aired around the ironing stove or kitchen range. Even I learned how to iron handkerchiefs! There were no drip-dry materials.

Reevsie came again on Thursday to scrub the rather rough stone floors of the dairy, kitchen, passage and back-kitchen. She used the water left in the furnace on Monday and it was slightly warmed up. This was only part of a day's work but I think she was given another meal and sometimes stayed longer.

On Saturday, my mother cooked a joint, two veg. and appropriate sauce and provided a sweet to follow. She prepared meals for Sunday and possibly for a day or two into the next week. Sunday was as far as possible, a day of rest.

When farm work was heavy she used to feed hens and collect eggs in the afternoon and sometimes shut up the hens at night. Every week there were eggs to be washed for collection on Mondays. It was she who set broody hens on nests of 13 eggs and looked after them. Every day the eggs were sprinkled with water and turned over while the hen was made to stretch her legs. When the chicks hatched, each 'family' was taken to a coop from which, in daytime, the chicks could run free and return to the shelter of the hen's wings and be shut up safely during hours of darkness.

There were also seasonal jobs. Every winter a pig was killed on the premises. The same day its "innards" were removed and there was fried liver and onions for dinner! Some offal was given away. The next day the butcher came back and cut the pig into joints. Some pieces were given away, some made into pork pies while large joints were cured for ham and bacon. This curing was heavy work and Dad did it till Oliver was strong enough to cope, but my mother always made the pickle according to an old family recipe. After some weeks these large joints were sufficiently cured and put in cotton bags and hung from hooks, some in the kitchen and some in what had been the cheese room a century earlier. How we all enjoyed the few weeks when roast meat was all pig-meat and not the usual beef or mutton!

In the autumn there were plum puddings to be made and these were boiled in the back kitchen furnace, for there were lots of them as, at Christmas, each worker was given one, large or small, according to the size of his family. A few puddings were also given as gifts to folk in the village who were either too poor or too old and feeble to make their own. This happened only between the two wars, as dried fruit could not be obtained during war years. Harvest teas have been mentioned elsewhere.

In season, jam, jelly and pickles were made from wild or home grown produce. My mother loved being out of doors and delighted in taking us bairns blackberrying or mushrooming and she spent any time she could spare helping in the large garden.

Should any of my readers be surprised by my use of the word "bairns", I must remind them that my father had spent nearly a year in Scotland and tell them that my mother had had a term at a boarding school at Inverness. Her eldest sister, Margaret, was on the staff there at the time of her twenty first birthday and as a present the Head Mistress said that for one term one of her sisters might attend the school free of charge. Eleanor was chosen as she was the eldest who could travel half price on the railway. She was taken to Birmingham and, with oversight of the guard, travelled alone to Edinburgh where she was met by Margaret, who organised the rest of the journey north. Margaret was never able to afford to go home for holidays, except once a year and then it was for the long summer break.

Margaret's further career is interesting. One day the Headmistress called a special staff meeting after tea and told the mistresses that times were changing and if they wanted careers in teaching they should get further qualifications. Margaret was the only one to take this advice and she went to study at the new

Teacher Training College in Cambridge. Though not officially part of the University, much help was given by University staff, male and female. Afterwards Margaret went on to a long career in the well-known St. George's School in Edinburgh.

There were seasonal pies to be made. I never liked rabbit pie or rook pie or lamb's tail pie.

Of course it was not possible to be completely self-sufficient and some food was delivered. Two bakers each called twice a week. Meat, ordered by postcard early in the week, was delivered on Friday. Some groceries could be bought in the village but our main supply came from the town. On alternate Tuesday afternoons a man cycled out from Alcester and took orders which were delivered on the following Friday. Transport was by horse and dray, which in wet weather was covered by a tarpaulin sheet. Little of the goods were pre-packed as they are today and polythene had not yet been invented, so, in wet weather, biscuits and other "dry" provisions did not always arrive in prime condition.

On dark winter evenings my parents were not too tired to play games with us, as we progressed from Snap, through Happy Families and Newmarket and lots of other games to Whist. Newmarket was scored with beans not real money. Dad was a very good reader and often read to us working our way from Grimm and Andersen to English classics. Meanwhile my mother sat mending and darning socks. She herself had a tremendous vocabulary and a good memory and excelled in telling us tales she had read or from English history.

On occasions she had to deal with emergencies. More than once I saw a weakly newborn lamb brought to the kitchen. There she wrapped it in a bit of old blanket and put it in a cool oven with its head by the open door. As it revived, it was fed with drips of warm milk until well enough to be returned to the fold or perhaps it had to be brought up as a pet lamb.... And I have seen her put splints on the leg of a lamb which had met with an accident. She always kept a supply of rolled bandages made from old sheets and thumb and finger stalls made from old gloves... for men met with accidents too.

When working with a steam saw, a man cut off the end of his thumb and came to the house for treatment. The end was hanging by a thread of skin. My mother packed it all together and Dad rushed him to Worcester for treatment and all seemed as well as could be... but this was before the days of tetanus injections. He suffered greatly but his life was saved and Worcester Royal Infirmary was greatly praised, as he was believed to be the first person ever to recover from tetanus.

On another occasion, a man, who was delivering cattle cake and had a heavy load on his back, slipped on a piece of mangold on the stone floor of the barn and fell flat on his face. He was brought to the house with terrible nose bleed and sat in the kitchen till she had staunched the flow.

At this time my mother had not been to any First Aid classes, but worked by traditional methods and "scowl of brow". In later years she did attend classes.

When we were small she found time to take us out and show us which berries and plants were poisonous and to teach us country lore including the cure for nettle stings which went like this: find a dock leaf, spit on it and rub the wet leaf on the sting.

With all the years of hard work she had done, it is not surprising that hands that in youth had done such beautiful drawn thread work had, in old age, become so gnarled and worn – and that sometimes when she tried to use them she cried out, "Oh my poor hands."

No children can have had better parents than ours and I thank God for them.

2.

EDUCATION, EDUCATION, EDUCATION!

In September 1922 I was launched into school life. Happily I rode my bicycle into Evesham and no thought ever crossed my mind that my work might not be up to the standard expected. I was right not to worry for I found myself well up in all subjects except French. The others in my class had had several years teaching from someone who was an expert and I think she was half French. In the whole of my life I have never recovered from the accent taught me by governesses who had never been to France and whose teachers had probably never been to France either. In those days there were no discs or tapes. When from time to time Governments decide that all primary school children should learn a foreign language, they seem to have no idea what harm may be done if a sufficient number of linguists has not already been recruited!

At the first scripture lesson, the mistress announced that this year we were going to study the Catechism and already I felt enough at home to announce that I was a Baptist and could not learn the Catechism, so I was given Scripture verses instead.

The other girls all knew how to play netball, but no-one ever told me the rules. I soon found out that you must not run with the ball but, as I had no jump in me, I rarely touched it. The next year we all started hockey. Hurrah!

At the end of the term before I arrived, the others in my class had started studying a long poem. We were given some of it as dictation and so I wrote down…

> "Just then a scout came flying,
> "All wild with haste and fear….."

and many more lines. I pictured a Boy Scout and it was a long time before I understood what the poem was about! I criticise this point but, on the whole, the teaching was well done and imaginative. How I enjoyed "Idylls of the King" and the History of Evesham.

For the first three terms I stayed Monday to Friday with my cousins and this was a very happy arrangement. After school, on sunny afternoons in the summer, Di and I often went to the swimming baths and I learnt to swim. Before that I had only bathed in the "Mill Pound" near my home.

But my thoughts stray back to the first Friday afternoon. I cycled home in bright sunshine and when I had about two miles still to go I saw a bicycle coming towards me and lo! It was Dad come to welcome me home! What a lot of news I had to relate. In those days many hedges still had rows of perry pear trees growing in them. In autumn the leaves of these trees turned a wonderful dark red and for the next few weeks I gloried in the view of them.

During the terms that followed I was a weekly boarder. Schoolwork progressed steadily and there was lots of time for fun and games with other boarders and this included dormitory feasts. We were never caught! I remember waking one night when the moon was shining brightly. So I crept out of the room, along a passage, through three classrooms, down a flight of stairs and let myself out through the day girls' door – no key, only bolted on the inside. Then I was free. There were no leaves on the beech trees and the shadows of branches danced in the moonlight. So I danced too. All was silent. There were no cars, no street lights, no house lights and I had no idea what time it was. In due course I retraced my steps safely and neither girls nor staff ever knew what a wonderful time I had had!

At Christmas 1924 I left this school but still have happy memories of my time there. I even remember the carol we sang at my last assembly. It was "Once in Royal David's City".

The next term I was at Alcester Grammar School, where Oliver was already installed. The boys from the village travelled there by bicycle but I joined a group of girls who went in a hired car, sometimes as many as seven of us in a four-seater!

I now set my mind on studying hard and getting some qualifications, so often I insisted on sitting up late doing homework. At this time I stopped growing and now wonder if there was any connection.

No need to describe grammar school life, for everyone can imagine this. By the time I was fourteen and a half I had decided, not only that I wanted to go to university, but that I would study science, as no girl from this school had already done so, though many boys had. I was allowed to study trigonometry and electricity/magnetism instead of needlework. A year later I could have changed my mind, but decided not to do so and eventually went into the sixth to do physics and chemistry as principal subjects with maths and French as subsidiaries. In the second year I was the only one doing this course and I do not think the science master took me very seriously! In due course the examination came and so did the results which were not considered good enough to warrant a third year in the sixth form in the hope of getting a university scholarship. At this point it seems that all decisions about my future were taken by other people and it was decided that I should go on to university at once and there was a vacancy at Reading.

By this time Oliver had done a short course in agriculture at Reading and Joyce was following me up the school but on the Arts side.

So in October 1930 I found myself at Reading University and, as all places in halls of residence had been filled, I was living with an uncle's family.

The next three years I was in a hall and made friends with a whole new group of people who were also working for science degrees. We worked hard at lectures, in labs, in the library in the mornings from 9am. till nearly 1pm., and in the afternoons from 2pm. to 5pm., except on Wednesdays and Saturdays. In winter I played hockey and in summer went cycling or swimming, though many people took up rowing or sculling. Mine was a good choice, as it was far more useful in my career than water sports would have been.

I make a few notes about the university in my day, so different from now. The number of students was, I think, six hundred plus, not the thousands who use the splendid new campus. Nearly all worked very hard as the economic climate was at a low ebb and parents were struggling to pay our fees.

The halls had strict rules. Meals were formal and dinner could only be missed ten times a term, even then we had to sign out and state where we were going and be in by 10pm. As we came out of the dining hall we were faced by a large framed piece of manuscript writing. Boldly it said, "I DO NOT EXPECT TO PASS" followed by more in smaller script. I never had the inclination to read the rest of it. What psychology! I wonder if it is still there! As we left our studies on Friday mornings, there, just outside the gate was an organ grinder with instrument and monkey greeting us with cheerful tunes. Those who could afford it threw down a penny! It reminded me of one of the songs Dad used to sing to us, a song he had learnt in kindergarten many years earlier.

"My master grinds an organ
And holds me by a chain
And when I pick the money up
You laugh and shout again

...but I wish I was in Monkey Land
the place where I was born."

At last the day came when degree results would be posted on notice boards at 3 p.m. I felt I couldn't hang about all day waiting for them, so arranged with a friend to get my result and put a note in my room, while I took my bicycle and in the glorious June weather spent a memorable day on the Berkshire Downs. I got back to find the note saying, "Honours, 2nd class." This was better than I expected for throughout the last two years maths had been a terrible trial to me. I hurried to send a telegram home....my parents came to Degree Day. With our new caps and gowns we had to wear black dresses and black shoes and stockings. With no money to spare I wore a borrowed dress and hockey stockings! I doubt if many of the new graduates could afford photographs.

A glorious long vacation followed.

I think this was the year of the mushroom! Though it may have been the next year. There was an enormous crop of wild field mushrooms on land that had been arable and now put down to grass. A college friend was staying with us and each day, at the crack of dawn, we set out with knives and baskets to cut those that had grown since yesterday and to work with a few others till about 7.45am. when all chip baskets were stacked into a car-drawn trailer and we went home to a breakfast of fried bacon and mushrooms. While we ate, my mother removed any broken mushrooms and weighed the chips, which were soon repacked in the trailer and delivered to Evesham market by 10 a.m. A fresh supply of chips was brought back ready for the next day's cutting. Of course, this abundance of mushrooms lasted only a few weeks.

Then back to Reading for a year doing teacher training. Most of my old pals were there doing similar courses, or perhaps a higher degree or repeating a failed one.

A short psychology course was very interesting and I have often wondered why this was left till after our degrees…for no-one had ever told me about the learning process. The Lent term was devoted to teaching practice and I was put down to go to a senior school in Reading. However, fortunately for me, though not for him, a grammar school science master at a mixed school was taken ill and myself and a biology graduate were sent to cover general science while he was away. Already two arts graduates were to go there, so every morning four of us set out by train. This was a wonderful opportunity for me, but as, after about a month, the science master recovered, I feared I should be sent back to the senior school… but then the maths master's wife was taken seriously ill and I switched on to my third subject. This was a wonderful experience, but most of the time I was without an experienced teacher to advise me.

I have never heard of another school where the headmaster ate school dinner every day and who carved for the whole school. All the time he was carving, one of the kitchen staff was sharpening a spare carving knife on the dining room doorstep. The

Head told me he was keen to keep an eye on the quality of food supplied and its cooking.

This was a happy term and I really felt I was working at last. We were all collecting testimonials and taking an interest in the Times Educational Supplement. In June I said "Goodbye" to Reading University, though I have visited the old buildings and the new campus in recent years.

Some years earlier I had started calling my parents King and Queen, and to this they made no objection. It was a happy arrangement and when college friends visited some also addressed them thus – less formal than Mr. and Mrs. Many years later I read in a psychology book that children who have great respect for their parents sometimes think of them as Emperor and Empress. What clumsy words!

3.

READY AND WILLING TO WORK

Yes, ready and willing to work, but first one had to find a job! For three years I had been one of many who had been given an education grant on promising to teach for at least two years when qualified. The school leaving age was to have been raised and it was expected that lots of extra teachers would be needed but, because of the recession, the leaving age had not been raised and there was no work for folk like me. Many of the advertisements said "Two years experience essential". Of course there were private schools where one might perhaps gain two years experience. Many of these were unrecognised and paid ninety pound a year resident. No suitable work was forthcoming till December when I did three weeks supply teaching in a Worcestershire elementary school, work for which I had been ill prepared. I had a class of nearly forty eight-year-olds for all subjects. I myself had never attended an elementary school or had any training for this age group..... but we all survived!

Many schools were now teaching general science instead of two separate subjects and I had no qualification in either botany or zoology, so in September, I signed on for evening classes at Worcester in biology and German. On Wednesdays and Saturdays I played hockey for Evesham Ladies and Monday afternoons went to Women's Institute dress-making classes, all of which stood me in good stead in the years to come. It entailed a hundred miles cycling a week. Between the wars if any of us were out cycling after dark, my mother put a lighted candle in the scullery window to welcome us home. The light of that candle could be seen from a distance of half a mile.

I applied for a hundred and fifty one posts before I got my first position. In January I was resident in a

Benedictine convent school, where the classes were small and there were no out-of-school duties, all of which were undertaken by nuns. The convent was enclosed and some of the older members had not been off the premises for fifty or more years! The grounds were extensive and beautiful. Many of the girls came from Ireland and shortly before St. Patrick's Day received packets of shamrock. Irish money circulated within the school and had to be sorted at end of term. The standard of maths, especially among the Irish, was very low, but I don't think anyone expected anything else, as many of them came from families more at home on the open field than in class-rooms....but there was one girl who was brilliant and who spoke excellent English, French, and German as well as her native Portuguese. From her I learnt some methods for arithmetic that I have found nowhere else.

The nuns were kind and delightful. There was no pressure on me to attend their church and on Sunday mornings I walked round the grounds with a nun who helped me with German conversation and in the afternoon I walked about a mile by field paths or road, according to weather, to a Methodist Chapel, which had previously been of the primitive persuasion.

There I was made very welcome and each week stayed to tea with three worthy sisters who also entertained the visiting preacher. So I was also able to go to the evening service. I much appreciated the friendship of these kind folk and enjoyed the good simple food they provided, for the convent food was monotonous in the extreme.

The five terms I was there taught me a lot. Never before had I considered the true meaning of "holiday" and "recreation". There was no pressure of work and I had time to explore the lovely countryside of Warwickshire on foot and on bicycle and to apply for more suitable jobs!

There were times when I wanted to explore further afield than could be managed in an afternoon by bicycle. So then I booked supper, bed and breakfast and lunch pack, (total cost 3s 6d) at a Youth Hostel where I hoped to meet a cheery group of young folk. One weekend was memorable but not for the reasons I anticipated.

Leaving the convent as soon as my morning commitments allowed, I set off light-heartedly and in due course arrived at my chosen hostel, where, alas, no-one else had booked for that particular night, so I spent the evening alone in a spooky sort of place.

Even the warden did not live there. Fortunately I am the sort of person who does not mind being alone.

After a good night's sleep I set off on a morning journey of exploration of the district and turned for 'home' soon after midday. By three o'clock the sun was hidden behind storm clouds and thunder rumbled in the distance. The storm came closer, but as yet there was no rain. Soon forked lightning reached the earth in fields around me and thunder roared. There was I on a bicycle, made of course of metal, and no shelter was in sight. As I knew there was a village about a mile ahead, I hurried on and soon came to a cottage where I asked for shelter till the storm passed. I was welcomed and my bike was put in a shed. Within minutes the skies opened and rain descended in torrents. Armed with a broom, the man of the house struggled to hold back water flowing in along a flagstone passage. The storm did not last long, but long enough for me to drink tea with the family. Then, thanking them for their kindness, I left and went on my way without further incident.

Times change. Recently when I have recounted this story, listeners have said, "Do you mean they really took you in as a stranger?" and similar remarks. I think they would do well to follow Cromwell's advice to his soldiers, whom he told to "Trust in God and keep your powder dry".

Now this happened in a year, (1936 I think), when there were many thunder storms but few as fierce as the one described, though we were used to being awakened in the night. Tired and happy I slept peacefully that night and came to breakfast saying to other lay staff how wonderful it had been to have had a night undisturbed by thunder. They looked at me in amazement and told me there had been a gigantic storm, and that lightning had been running down all the convent lightning conductors. As soon as the storm had abated, people had come from the village to see if the nuns were all right and to render any help that might be necessary!

Before the War, outside many cottages there were notices saying, "Teas" and here cyclists knew they would find a welcome. On one of my cycling trips out from the convent, I decided to sample one of these and was indeed made most welcome. Sitting at a table by a window with a view down a neat garden, I was provided with several slices of neatly cut bread and butter, a dish of home-made jam, slices of slab cake as well as a pot of tea with sugar and milk. I asked for and paid the bill which was 10d and was about to mount my bicycle and ride away, when the woman came running down the path and said," I see you didn't take milk and sugar, so here is a halfpenny back." I would be surprised if anything like that happened today.

Shortly before I left the convent I had an indirect invitation, brought to me by one of the lay staff, that I should be warmly welcomed if I wished to join the community as a novice. My decision would have been the same even if I had not already accepted a post at another school.

After an interview in London, when I was given to understand that the school was likely to be "recognised" shortly, I went to another private school, this time in Margate. Here classes were small, so marking was light, but out-of school duties took much time. Every fourth day started at seven thirty a.m. inspecting teeth and finger nails in dormitories and finished at nine p.m. when all dormitory lights were out. Again the food was poor and I remember a day, when not on duty, I was so hungry after school dinner that I got on my bike, rode into town, propped the bike outside Lyons, went in, ordered and ate a poached egg on toast (four old pence.) and got back to school for afternoon lessons! Living in a town was much more expensive than in a convent and of course fares for travelling home for holidays were significant and my salary had gone down by £5 a year.

Living by the sea was a great novelty, but the winds were very cold and sometimes in the winter it was difficult to persuade the girls to remove their gloves to do written work. However in the summer, there was swimming and, on half day holidays, duty consisted of taking boarders for picnics on the beach.

I soon began to attend evening classes at Thanet School of Art and enjoyed this immensely but, of course, my attendance was very irregular because of duty days. The work we did was extremely interesting to me….and lo and behold, I soon found myself teaching junior art as well as maths. Financially the school was in a very bad way and this saved paying a professional art teacher for several hours a week. Attendance at art school made me miss staff suppers but I much preferred to queue for "small fish and one of chips, salt and no vinegar" at a shop I passed on the way back. The cost was 4d., but sometimes I was extravagant and had "two of chips".

I carried this back wrapped in newspaper and ate it in the school cellar.

In my second year I made friends with the new Ma'm'selle but this I record elsewhere.

Sundays here were very different from those at the convent. On duty one went to church talking to the Head and walking at the back of a crocodile of girls wearing white gabardine uniform dresses. We arrived very early for the Head liked us to be sitting demurely when the other schools came in. Why? I wonder. I confess I used mentally to put numbers on the hymn board into prime factors and I think some of the pupils did too. After school dinner, the girls wrote home and the duty mistress was supposed to check what and how they had written. I don't think I ever did this job properly. In fine weather a long walk followed and once the older girls led us to a well-hidden quarry where, they told me, dissenters had worshipped to avoid persecution in days long gone. I was never able to find this quarry again!

When not on duty, I went on Sunday mornings to the Baptist chapel. The first week I was shown to a pew and afterwards treated it as my own, although it was labelled with someone's name. I never saw this person, who perhaps attended only in the evening.

No-one spoke to me until the last week that I was in Margate, and then the minister's wife enquired where I was living.

Sometimes, when not on duty, I leapt on my bicycle and cycled the seventeen miles into Canterbury, propped the bike against the Cathedral wall and attended Evensong – always a small congregation, so everyone sat in the choir stalls and enjoyed the beautiful service. When I came out the unchained bicycle was still there, waiting to carry me back. In those days no-one considered that it might someday be otherwise.

A few years later I did appreciate the possibility, for I was now working in Cheshire and Yanks were stationed nearby. An acquaintance left her bike propped against the pavement and went into a shop. When she came out the bicycle had gone but the basket had been removed from the handlebars and left on the pavement. In it was a note saying that a G.I. had urgent need of a bike, so here's £10, buy yourself a new one and there was a £10 note! Not everyone who "lost" a bicycle was so lucky!

How did I come to live in Nantwich? After two

years at Margate, it was time to move. The employment situation had eased somewhat but, sometime after my appointment, the school secretary told me there had been over a hundred applications for the job, so I wondered how I had at last been selected to serve in a school where I already felt at home. I had a junior post in a mixed grammar school in a country town. At the interview the head asked if I would be able to take over a book binding club. I told him honestly that I knew nothing about book binding but was attending the Thanet School of Art several evenings a week, that there was a book binding department and I thought they might let me move into that for the last seven weeks of term. This proved to be the case and I was given a complete course of elementary book binding, which interested me greatly and was sufficient for a school club. I cannot praise too much the help and encouragement I was given by the Art School, as I must have been a nuisance to some of the staff.

So in September 1938, I was in the job for which I had yearned. My timetable put me in charge of all the maths and general science in the first year of Grammar School and a share of these subjects in the second year – and senior hockey. I had useful help and advice from a science master who had been at Reading not too many years before I was there and an excellent laboratory assistant made life easy.

The senior mistress had found me comfortable digs, sharing a sitting room with a new French mistress who had also been at Reading with me. Wonderful food! What a change! I think my salary was £240 per annum.

The first year slipped away happily. I soon discovered how friendly Northerners were compared with those who dwelt in the South. I was welcomed at the Baptist Church, which was a nice change, and I always sat with Miss Fitton who came from the same family as the "Dark lady of the Sonnets". I still correspond with people who were teenagers on that first Sunday and who are now stalwarts of the church.

The book binding club flourished and gradually I came to realise that the keenest members came from A-forms who did Latin instead of any form of handwork. Over the years I have come to the conclusion that young folk can be pushed into academic channels too early. The club lasted many years and only began to decline when timetables were arranged so that all could do some handwork if they desired.

At the beginning of the term when I arrived in Cheshire, the brine swimming pool had not yet closed for winter and this delighted me. There was a whole new countryside to explore and some staff, who also loved the open air, showed me their favourite haunts. With several of my new friends, I joined a Workers' Educational class on international affairs.

Please don't think that lesson preparation and marking were neglected!

Looking back from the twenty first century, I realise how different things were before the Second World War. Then there were no married women teachers and the single women were paid far less than men doing the same work. There was social life for the staff so we got to know each other well.

So a year slipped away and before we returned the next autumn, war had broken out. Every one had to carry gas masks and each Monday, what had been a rather casual form period was now devoted to gas mask inspection. As soon as any mask had been inspected, it was supposed to be worn for the rest of the period. What a hope!

Then there was an edict that the inside of all windows was to be covered with muslin gauze pasted in place to avoid splintering in the event of air attacks. Each class was responsible for its own room and I had a class of 11–12 year-olds in a room, two walls of which were almost entirely glass. I guess I was not the only relieved teacher, when two of the more senior boys found that they enjoyed the work involved and in dinner hours and any time available dealt with nearly all the windows in the school.

Soon fire watching was organised and each night three staff and three sixth formers were on duty. The young folk had camp beds on the stage with curtains drawn, making a snug room. Arrangements were made for staff to have beds at three strategic spots and to do three-hour shifts but pupils were not disturbed unless there was an alert, when all six were on duty. Soon it was decided that only the staff need be present and before the end of the war, that number was cut to two. I don't think anyone ever had to do anything! On winter evenings we sat in the domestic science room beside the range with a pleasant coal fire. The school had a most excellent cook who sent us good meals which had only to be heated. There were advantages for when rationing started, these meals were free of coupons.

The school stood at the end of the fire-watchers'

beat and sometimes they dropped in to sit by our fire. I remember an occasion when one of them cast an eye over walls and ceiling and said, "A lot of heavy masonry here to fall on you girls if there's a raid." There were alerts but no raids. So what was the snag? In the depth of winter there was very little time between the end of afternoon school and the beginning of fire watching. So folk did not leave the school between 9 a.m. one day and 4 p.m. the next, with two days' work between. The rota continued, every fourth night, through term and holidays and this meant a lot of swapping, so that staff who lived a long way from school could get several consecutive nights. Of course when groups were reduced in size from three to two the duty became less frequent, but food and conditions deteriorated.

For a short time we received evacuees from a boys' Grammar School on Merseyside. Two of their masters joined our staff and some others came down for odd times to keep their exam work going. Timetables were reorganised and I had a class of their second formers for chemistry. On one occasion I was demonstrating an experiment when the flask in my hand exploded! There was I, standing quite unharmed among shattered glass..... but where were the boys?

Under the benches, for they had experienced air raids and knew more about explosions than I did.

In the early days of 1940 there was sharp frost for some weeks. After school, lots of pupils and some staff cycled to a lake about two miles distant and skated. At full moon this was splendid, but even at other times, there were often a few cars with dimmed headlights trained across the ice. I was a poor skater but managed to play ice hockey with my young pupils. Only once did I play in a senior game and then magnificently saved a goal by falling down across the path of the puck. I have no idea of the rules of the game but feel sure there ought to have been a penalty for this! Football and hockey were out of the question so, in senior games period, we took those who wished on to the frozen canal basin near the school for sliding and fun on a very rough surface. The sluggards stayed in and got on with their homework.

Soon the young men on the staff disappeared to army and airforce and were replaced by married women. My chance had come! I now taught junior and middle school maths, specialising in lower sets up to exam level. Following a brilliant mathematician I soon discovered that you can be far too good at maths to teach lower sets well. I learnt that every process must be broken down into minute steps, instead of saying halfway through the reasoning, "It now becomes obvious that x = 2.3" or whatever the right answer might be. This was a period when I was experimenting with the use of colour in geometry diagrams. The idea was not original but came from my predecessor at Margate, who was an Australian. Though I never met her, I saw some of the work she left: Does anyone else use colour? If not, why not! There is a snag, as you have to look out for colour blind boys. If I suspected anyone, I checked with the art master, who tested all pupils when they first came into school. I met only one boy who was completely colour-blind and then adapted the method for that set. How I envy today's staff who have white boards! But I would not like to be told how everything should be done with no room for experimentation.

Meanwhile staff came and went and I became House Mistress (not a very arduous task) and Guide Captain, which took a lot of time and effort but was enjoyable and, fifty years on, one of those Guides wrote and told me how much she had enjoyed it! I had enjoyed my Guiding days and made the mistake of writing my thesis for Education Diploma on

Guiding, and this was mentioned in my testimonial, so in three of the four schools where I taught I was roped in to run the school company. This took a lot of time, hikes, weekend camps with other companies, Guides Sports Day on our school field, Guiders' meetings and conferences and occasional training days!... all good fun but time consuming. In Cheshire our company had a "breakfast hike" each year when we arrived at school very early and cooked and ate a meal in a disused corner of the grounds and cleared it all up before morning school. This never caught on with the next and last company I had. At the time most county authorities moved pupils from primary to secondary schools at the age of eleven. I've often wondered if the Guide Movement appreciated that, when they changed the age at which Brownies moved up to Guides from eleven to ten, they would kill many day-school companies! Any girl who wanted to be a Guide was already enrolled somewhere else before coming to secondary school. I was present at the demise of two such companies. But some years before this happened, some of us younger staff thought that perhaps it was time our pupils became acquainted with youth hostels so, with the headmaster's permission, three of us arranged to take a group of fourth year girls for a weekend at Wilderhope Hostel. We took our bicycles by train to Shrewsbury, cycled to the hostel, slept in the haunted dormitory, but saw no ghost. We explored some of Shropshire, especially Stokesay, which the staff loved, but after a short survey, the girls asked permission to go and have a meal at a "British Restaurant"* they had seen about a mile away. Peace for the staff ! This was shortly before D-day. More cycling on Sunday and back by train. In those days a dozen or more bicycles could be taken by train, without pre-booking and without payment. On a later trip a guard helped load the bicycles and refused a tip, saying he was sure he earned more than I did! On that first trip I had been a little taken aback, when, just before we set out, the mother of one of the girls said that Annie suffered from rheumatism and must on no account get her knees wet! Fortunately it didn't rain. This was the first of more than a dozen hostel weekends for fourth year girls and we were usually given a day off school. Over the years we visited, not only Shropshire, but Derbyshire and Wales as well as the Lake District in an autumn half- term. Sometimes we simply had

**British Restaurant – One of a chain of restaurants.*

walking holidays instead of taking bicycles to hilly or mountainous districts.

Early in the war, 1940 I think, the W.V.S. began organising the collection of herbs for medicinal purposes. School children were asked to bring rosehips picked at the weekends in autumn. At morning break on Mondays I weighed them and kept account of how much each pupil had brought, for ultimately they would be paid. Hips were collected from school later in the morning. Was I mad when a girl brought in hips and haws mixed, as they had to be sorted! Cheshire was congratulated on the quality of the hips sent but, a couple of years later, we were told that no more were wanted, as they were deficient in vitamin C ! It was essential that hips should be processed within a day or two of picking and perhaps some of the Cheshire folk had not appreciated this fact.....

For a couple of years the W.V.S. also dried leaves of medicinal herbs in an airy loft near school and I, with a few second year boys, helped with this on Wednesday evenings. Those who picked the leaves had laid them singly on wire netting shelves. Every leaf had to be turned over each day. We were told that small bunches of young stinging nettles which, from time to time, were hanging from the ceiling need not be touched. They went mouldy. Ours not to reason why! We just got on with the job and after the first evening, when I was shown where the key was hidden, I do not think anyone came to see how we were getting on. This project did not last long and I suspect the English climate is not very good for herb drying. When the Americans came to Britain's aid, they were probably able to supply all the drugs needed.

What we did, cannot have been much help to the war effort, but was an activity in which staff and pupils could mix and gossip and share school jokes quite informally.

There were always lots of things going on in wartime. For some time I spent alternate Sunday evenings helping at a W.V.S. canteen for the forces. Sometimes this was a lot of fun, but one could be stuck at the sink with an inadequate supply of hot water and tea towels. As far as I know, no-one died or was even ill as a result of unhygienic conditions. In those days our immune systems were good!

For two seasons I helped with a Girls' Brigade in the town and the most interesting thing I did there was to teach soft toy making, using scraps of material left over from pre-war dressmaking – mine and other peoples!

For a short period I was a member of the Play Reading Circle, but that was not really my "thing", so I soon resigned. I was more at home with a little sketching group that went out on summer evenings. Once when I had had an insect bite at the corner of my eye, the eye was black. When we met and were waiting for the leader, I was ragged and asked who had attacked me. Below the babble, I heard a low voice say, "But who would do that to Little Miss Jackson?" hence the title of this book. In due course the Senior Mistress/Deputy Head retired and for better or worse, I was appointed in her place. This was not an arduous job, as the headmaster liked to do everything himself.

In 1960 the school celebrated its 400th anniversary and it fell to my lot to entertain the Duchess of Gloucester in my room for a short rest period between lunch, given by the Chairman of Governors, and the afternoon ceremony when she would present the prizes. I had not previously considered the difficulty of guiding someone about a building when protocol demanded walking two steps behind the person being led.

Meanwhile things were changing down in Worcestershire. Oliver had married a landgirl and was living with his wife and two daughters in a farm cottage. In 1957 Dad decided to have a small home for retirement built on the farm, so that the young family could move into the old farmhouse, my mother would have less work and he a smaller garden. When I was home for spring half-term the walls were about three courses high and I well remember the sunny Sunday afternoon when I sat on them and regretted the loss of good agricultural land. I looked around at the Perry Mill ground and thought of days gone by when the field was not only cow pasture but a children's playing field. Over there Dad and I had tried, very unsuccessfully, to fly a kite I had been given. We decided it was a cheap kite and no good! Across there he had tried to teach Oliver and me to dribble and pass a football. At the bottom of the field we had our cricket pitch, so often in use in long summer holidays when the house had been full of cousins and school friends. Oh! the days gone by!

At Easter the building was almost finished and when I came "home" at Whit and found some of the dear old furniture and pictures in new rooms, I felt quite happy and it has been my home ever since.

Mains electricity came in 1957 just as the building was being finished, but there was no mains water for another year and all drinking water had to be carried from the old farm well.

I began to think of coming home to live with my ageing parents and looked for advertisements of suitable posts in Worcestershire. Times had changed, for now there was little competition, so in the summer term 1964 I started work at Redditch High School, where one of my friends was senior mistress and helped me to settle into my new job. Of course, no school could ever be like the one where I had worked for about a quarter of a century.

I regretted having left my old flat, only half a mile from school, but soon adapted to using a school bus, which was free to staff in Worcestershire but would not have been available to them in Cheshire. However I soon found that more often than not I was driving my own car, for yet again, I was Guide Captain and not much later House Mistress. It was good to pick up friendships with folk who had been at school with me and of course I was known through my parents, who, over many years, had been active in the community. My mother was a founder member of the Women's Institute and later its president. She was on the committee that worked behind the local Girl Guides and she had been appointed (by a C.of E. Committee I think) to look after the welfare of boarded-out children. From time to time she sat all night at the bedside of one or another old parishioner, so that the usual carer (voluntary) could get a proper night's rest. For many years Dad was chairman of the School Managers, Treasurer of the Nursing Association and of the Gymkhana Fund, which eventually produced money for an Army hut and then a village hall and he was an active member of the Farmers' Union. Though a Baptist he was often asked to read a "lesson" at the Anglican Church on occasions of national significance and at Rogationtide. Both worked with great dedication for the Community Council. I am amazed at the amount of energy they had for good works when I think of all the long hours they spent on farm, garden and housework.

Soon I found myself proposed and elected to the Parish and Community Councils, but with new work in a new school and with ageing parents I could not give the necessary time and only served for a short while.

My mother became ill and a kind friend, a retired nurse, came every school-day to get her washed and dressed in the morning. Their Diamond Wedding was celebrated, but was a very tame affair compared with their Golden Wedding, when many relations of their generation had been well enough to travel long journeys to be with them. The following January Mother died and Dad was very sad and lonely. For me life became tougher. At that period home-helps and maths teachers were equally scarce. We already had a good help but had only got her when I had pointed out to the "powers-that-be" that if one couldn't be found there would be more than a hundred and fifty grammar school pupils without maths teaching. Unfortunately the help couldn't cook, so I had to prepare Dad's midday meals, though he was capable of cooking vegetables for himself. Sister Joyce and her husband were very kind and, of their fortnight's summer holiday, spent a week here, thus allowing me a week away from home. We used to play Scrabble nearly every evening and sometimes I didn't start marking and lesson preparation till 10p.m. and in the morning I had to make sure that Dad was up and able to cope with cooking his breakfast. In this period Dad had a fall which necessitated dressings on his leg, so the District Nurse, known to many as Hawk-Eye, came regularly to attend to this and she has been my friend ever since.

I retired at the end of the summer term before my sixtieth birthday and I'm glad I did, as this gave me the autumn at home with Dad, who died the following January.

I scarcely knew what to do with my freedom!

4.

EDUCATION FAR AND WIDE

In every country I visit I try, as far as possible, to take an interest in its education system. I remember a scorching hot day in Barcelona, when, instead of siesta, I walked about the almost deserted streets and looked in the windows of closed shops. Suddenly I found an open shop, a large cool bookshop. So in I went and gravitated to the section with school textbooks and looked at lots of junior maths books. I was amazed to find that pupils were learning not only the old traditional Spanish measures and the metric system but also English weights and measures, presumably for purposes of trade, for we had not then "gone metric". I bought a copy of one of these books. Later, at the end of a summer term, my twelve to thirteen year old pupils, who were bright and learnt Latin and who were well up with their maths, were told about Barcelona and I wrote carefully selected questions on the board. I hope they enjoyed coping with a language they hadn't met before.

I wonder why foreign languages teaching in our schools seems, nearly always, to be geared to French and / or German. Surely there are more people in the world who speak Spanish than either and lower sets would find it easier to learn.

The scene changes. The sun shines. I am sitting alone on a seat and watching the Seine flow quietly by and behind me stands Notre Dame. An elderly gentleman comes and sits at the other end of the seat and soon asks if I am Dutch or does he say Deutsche? In any case the answer is the same. We talk. I teach junior science in an English lycée. He is senior chemistry master in a French lycée. Would I like to see his lab? We walk a short distance. He takes out a large bunch of keys and unlocks the school and then the laboratory. There appears to be lots of apparatus, but packed tidily away in glass-fronted cupboards. I am lost for suitable words. The one thing I shall always remember is the colour of the walls which were darkish grey and shiny – practical but so depressing. We come out into the sunshine and he takes me to see a small church. Then we sit and drink the best fruit juice I have ever tasted. A pleasant afternoon and we have not spoken one word of English!

Shortly after I took up my last teaching post, I was invited to join a school party to Germany and thus, for ten days or so, I was an official guest of the City of Cologne. This really only meant that I had a free pass on all public transport. I was billeted with a family who had a fifteen-year-old daughter and I spent one morning visiting her school. It was splendidly neat and well-furnished, no shortage of books or equipment, pupils' uniform and behaviour impeccable and only about twenty pupils in a class. I was able to listen to two lessons. One was history and at the end of it I knew more about the Treaty of Vienna than I had ever known before. This was largely a lecture by the teacher. The other was an English lesson, very practical. Looking back I wonder if this was a fee-paying school.

Planning a second holiday at a small resort on the

east coast of the Peloponnesos, I wrote, in my best Linguaphone Greek, to the head of the primary school there and asked if I might visit it. No reply. So I went and called and was told I could come the following morning. School starts early, (7.30a.m.) finishes about 1pm and in that time there are two breaks. I arrived during the first break and was met by a mistress on playground duty. I don't think she had been warned I was coming as she ran in to ask about it. Break over we went into her classroom, where she taught two years together, average age perhaps seven. This meant she had a class of sixty in a room built for thirty. Desks were pushed together in pairs and, there being one pupil absent, I shared what amounted to a double desk with one of the boys. The front row of desks was so close to the blackboard that there was scarcely room to turn round and I am sure those in front corner desks could not see the writing on the board. The first lesson was Greek language and very interesting to me, but so dull. None of the pupils showed any sign of life, no-one asked a question. I think this lesson lasted an hour.

Then came the second break. My new friend ran in and got us cups of coffee to drink while we did playground duty and she told me more about the school. She was the only mistress on the staff and the only one who had a double sized class. The head master had a class of eleven pupils who were potential scholarship winners. She had no free periods and taught her class for all subjects, including music, handicrafts and PE. I studied the timetable carefully and asked how she managed music and was told she just put on records. There was no sign that she ever took home any marking. I glanced at the written work they had done in arithmetic and it seemed they marked their own or perhaps occasionally each others. I was not surprised that this mistress was hoping to change her job soon.

Of course one must not judge a school on one short visit, nor a country's educational system by one provincial school.

In the same town we saw a crocodile of small children coming from an outlying building. On enquiry they proved to be returning from a French kindergarten and were no doubt fee paying pupils. We discovered there was also an English kindergarten and no doubt the Germans had one too.

One afternoon I was sitting alone and a teenage girl came and asked politely if I was English and could she please come and talk to me and in this way got half an hours free English conversation. She attended a state secondary school in the mornings and her parents paid for special coaching privately.

A few years later, on a bus in Athens, I sat behind two ladies who had been buying new text books needed by their children for the coming term. They were laughing as they looked at junior modern maths books and were clearly saying that maths had changed since their young days!

When we booked a holiday in Karpathos, we imagined it to be a very poor island. On arrival, towards the end of the summer holidays, there were lots of young people about but the second week they seemed to have disappeared! We discovered that the juniors went by school bus to a town about twelve kilometres away and were back later in the day. But where were the secondary "students"? No-where to be seen. On enquiry we were told they had all gone to school in America and would be back for Christmas.

Long ago, when I taught junior science, I acquired a second hand book, the title and author of which I have forgotten, but it was an American production, full of lively stories about scientists and some of their discoveries and explanations of well-known facts. One such tale describes how, when walking up a steep mountain side when the sun is rising or setting directly behind him and there is a bank of white cloud above the skyline, a walker might see his own shadow on the cloud. In earlier days to see such an image of oneself was considered a portend of disaster or death. Even today many people seeing this for the first time are surprised or even terrified.

I personally have never seen this, but once, when I was with a tramping party in Yugoslavia, we had before us a climb, not long but steep in parts. One of our group had discovered he had no head for heights, so, with an elderly Croat, decided to come by a long circuitous route. We were all at the hut in good time and when it was beginning to get dark the young Englishman arrived, stumbling and talking incoherently, saying his elderly companion was so tired he was unable to walk. Within seconds every man in the hut had put on his boots and was racing down the path. Almost at once they met the Croat walking slowly but steadily. He was quite calm and collected. Apparently they had seen their shadows on the clouds and the effect on the young Englishman, who did not appreciate that there was a scientific explanation, was as dramatic as if he had been a medieval peasant.

On one occasion in Yugoslavia I was fortunate enough to be on a tramping tour led by Janko. He was a graduate and after his degree had specialised in teaching deaf and dumb children. Asked about this he gave all the right answers, how wonderful it was when a child looked at his mouth, felt his throat and began to make the same movements etc etc... After a pause he added "…. and of course you never have more than three in a class... and there's no marking!"

The scene was now a Colonie de Vacances somewhere in Alsace and the year 1948, soon enough after the war for English people to be welcomed warmly in France. I was there with a group of walkers at the same time as a school party of 10 – 12 year olds from north west France. As an opening gambit I set out to discover whether or not French children knew our game Noughts and Crosses and soon found that they didn't – but the ice was broken and whenever I came in, and they were not occupied, a group of a dozen or so gathered round me and delighted me by singing Breton folk songs.

For several years while I was in Cheshire, I ran a branch of "The Caravan", a negligible amount of work. It simply meant receiving small bundles of letters written by pupils in other countries and occasionally from older folk, all of whom wanted pen-friends in England. Most requests came from the U.S.A. so after reading many introductory letters written by teenagers there I formed an opinion of the standard of their education....but that was more than a generation ago!

Among the pen-friends not wanted by my pupils were two whom I decided to answer. One of these was a Russian man, older than I, who wanted to exchange postage stamps, preferably complete sets of British mint stamps. This proved expensive but well worth doing, because of the quiet, unwritten friendship one sensed. News exchanged was negligible, for example "It is very cold, the snow is one metre deep"...but I also received lots of picture post cards. This correspondence lasted about forty years till Vladimir died.

My other pen-friend was a Japanese girl in a

Roman Catholic school and her English was already good. A year or two later she decided to become a nun and would not be allowed to write during her novitiate – so that was that – or was it? A few years later she had become Sister Maria Beda and had permission to write, since when our correspondence has flourished and her English is well-nigh perfect, but I have learnt absolutely no Japanese. We now write freely on any subject that moves us and occasionally I have been able to help her. When she had to teach the history of the Second World War, she asked what I felt on D-day. The answer was simple, I didn't know it was D-day but I was able to put her in touch with some one who had been involved and now she has two English pen-friends! This friendship too must already have lasted more than forty years.

5.

SOME FRIENDSHIPS

While a teenager (we didn't use that term then) it was difficult for me to make much contact with fellow pupils outside school because of its distance from my home. Though, in the summer, a few of us sometimes swam in a lake not far from school and in winter, when conditions were right, we sometimes skated there.

But, when I was sixteen, I organised a cycling tour with Mary a "friend" who was in the same form. She had never visited my home or I hers. In the Easter holidays we explored the Rollright Stones on our way to the Cotswolds. In those days they seemed so lonely, so remote, so romantic. I have never again appreciated them so much. For two nights we stayed at Blockley with my former governess Cockie, who provided supper, bed and breakfast and lunch packs… and we explored many villages, including Stow-on-the-Wold and Bourton-on-the-Water. My map reading was not very good! I imagine some correspondence had previously gone on between our parents and with Cockie. At this time there were no youth hostels in England.

At University things were different. Lots of freshers from different places and backgrounds were thrown together and one soon found friends within a group of fellow students, who met in Hall, in labs. and in teams….but I made one friend on the eve of the first day of my first term. Called to a meeting, I was looking for the room, when I fell in with another on the same quest and so a lifelong friendship started! "Foote" and I had very different backgrounds. She was some years older than I, born in India, daughter of a high ranking army officer. It had always been assumed that she would marry into the army and that she would inherit money from her grandmother. Neither happened so, although very knowledgeable, she had no paper qualifications. She had gone to South Africa, worked in the Botanic Gardens in Johannesburg and, while there, had played hockey for that country. She treasured a newspaper cartoon, which labelled her, "The Springiest Springbok of them all"! Eventually it became necessary to have some qualifications, so she came to England to study biology and, after a 'gap' year to earn more funds, became a PhD and lectured at Achimota College.

It is amazing that we never quarrelled, but just accepted each other. Having had such different upbringings we disagreed on religion, politics and almost everything else, but remained friends to the end of her life. From time to time she descended upon me from some out-post of the former Empire and we spent some time together either at my flat or at home, where my parents welcomed her warmly. When she retired and lived in Sussex, I was able to visit her and we spent one specially happy summer day at Bateman's for she venerated Rudyard Kipling and treated the house and garden as her own.

Betty came to Reading a year after I did. We were on the same course and in the same hall of residence. Soon we became friends and have remained so for more than seventy years. She was far more active than I, as I discovered when we explored the Lake District together, for, by the time I was half way up a mountain side, she was sitting at the top laughing and ready to move on. In later years we visited each other from time to time, but while I explored Europe she went further afield, taking exchange jobs in America and Africa. On holiday she walked on the Great Wall of China and camped in Outer Mongolia.

After she retired Betty devoted herself to looking after a handicapped sister, which she did splendidly. At the age of eighty nine she enjoyed a trip to Antarctica. What next I wonder!

Here I must digress to show how I came to meet Ella, a German lady slightly older than myself. The year I took my degree, I decided to give myself a holiday and so scraped together enough to go to Germany. After family holidays ceased and before we were earning, my mother had given us children three pounds each, every year, to spend as we chose. That was a start. Grandpa J. had shares in a tea company and for many years had divided his dividends among his grandchildren's savings bank accounts, which he had opened. I withdrew all of mine, I forget how much it was, perhaps about ten pounds. So I booked a holiday with 'International Tramping Tours', which was non-profit making and run voluntarily by a group of Quakers as a contribution towards international friendship. Everything was of the simplest. Every tour had two leaders, of opposite sex, one English and the other of the country visited....I had a splendid holiday in the Eifel district of Germany. Many other I.T.T. holidays followed. In 1935, I was with I.T.T. in Somerset and Devon, the cheapest tour I could find (about £5 for a fortnight!). Ella from Frankfurt was on that tour. Of course we became close friends as she was an anglophile.

The following year I scraped together enough money to take my mother on holiday to Germany. After a fortnight at two centres in the Harz Mountains, we had a week-end in Frankfurt with Ella and her parents. Though they had no mutual language, the two mothers were happy to spend time together and understood each other well. Ella visited us in 1939, when war was in the air and even when we were alone in the Worcestershire countryside, she instinctively looked round to see if anyone was listening, before telling an anti-Nazi joke...

By the time we were in touch again, Ella's parents had died and she had married an Austrian with a very distinctive Slav surname and they had one son, Sepp. Soon afterwards a girl followed. She was called Ruthi and, by proxy, I was a Roman Catholic godmother. They were really terribly short of food, while I found it comparatively easy to send them monthly food parcels from what we thought were meagre rations.

In due course I was able to visit and meet the newcomers to Ella's family – but alas! the father was soon ill and died, leaving Ella to cope with a young family and a partly built house out in the country, a beautiful place where I stayed several times.

Ella, her children and sometimes a mutual friend managed to visit me occasionally. Young Sepp was brilliant, settled into a good teaching post and married. Ruthi also married and had two children. She and her husband and first child stayed a few days with me, so the friendship lasted into four generations.

A few years later, Ruthi stopped answering my letters and since then I have had no communication with the family. A mutual friend told me that disaster had struck young Sepp and that this had been reported in most of the newspapers. Because of the unusual Slav surname, there was no doubt about to whom the reports referred. The disaster was a misfortune not a disgrace and there was no need to have felt ashamed.

At the convent my chief friend was a kindly nun, who coached me in German conversation as we walked together through the grounds. It was an enclosed order and we therefore lost touch when I left.

During my second year at Margate, Denise was ma'm'selle. Both being internationally minded we soon became great friends. Suddenly a house quite close to the school became full of Spanish boys. Wishing to help, we knocked on the door and were greeted by two young Spanish school masters with adequate English, and I, who was struggling to learn Spanish at the time, asked if there was anyone who could help me. Yes, there was one young woman there, reputed to be sixteen years old, but I think a little older, who had two brothers among the boys. I was warned that her Spanish was not very good. So from time to time, taking my Spanish reader with me, I went for a lesson. My salary was minuscule and hers as "matron" non-existent, so each time only one shilling changed hands. This only lasted a short time, but occasionally Denise and I took her out. During that year how we knitted! Always boy's pullovers, whatever the size or colour it would fit someone!

We never knew how they came to be in Margate

nor what became of them finally. I always picture that, when "Potato" Jones ran the blockade into Bilbao harbour, he brought out a load of refugees – that's conjecture… but I do know that our activities were frowned upon by the principal of our school.

Denise spent Easter holidays at my home and in the summer I visited hers in central France and was made most welcome. Her father was postmaster of the town and also inspected telephones over a wide area. He had saved up inspections for some time and on alternate days took Madame, Denise and me out for long drives. Whenever we came to a telephone box we stopped and he inspected it thoroughly… and one Sunday, when he was not working, we went as far as Avignon and saw the town "en fête" and also went to the Pont du Gard. The next week we went to the Gorges du Tarn. But my clearest memory is of a very hot weekday when we came upon a group of "ouvriers de la ligne". Of course we stopped and there was some inspection and discussion. Monsieur had asked if there was a hostelry nearby where drink could be obtained. Faces brightened and in a moment the workers had piled on to their lorry and we were following them. We soon reached our destination. Inside a long cool room there was a long trestle table.

Monsieur sat at the head and was very jovial with the workmen, who looked worshipfully at him, as they drank at his expense. Meanwhile, at the lower end of the table, we three took our drinks in a ladylike manner.

Denise was at the University of Paris in the academic year that followed and at Easter I spent a few days in the British hostel in the Cité Universitaire. She, being French, could choose which hostel she liked and was established in the American one. In those few days she managed to show me many of the famous sights of the city and we sat in "the Gods" at ballet and opera. Everywhere there were rumours of war and lots of false coinage. In the University restaurant every coin was weighed.

War came and I had no news of my friend till it ended. By that time Denise had married a veterinary student from French Equatorial Africa and they had a son. Her father was now postmaster of the Paris XII district and they all lived in a good flat over the Post Office. Though the war had finished in the previous summer, I was unable to get a visa in April and by the time I went to Paris in the summer holidays, Denise and family had gone to Africa. I never saw Denise again. She had another son and soon afterwards died a most painful death after being carried many miles on a stretcher to hospital. However, my connection with the family was not lost. I learned that I was the first friend Denise had ever had and I was welcomed for her sake and for many years I had a home from home in Paris. All my conversation had been with Madame, who knew no word of English. Monsieur knew a lot, having worked with British troops during the First World War, but he never joined in the conversation, except that he would simply throw in an English word if we were completely stuck. Early during my post-war visit, Madame told me that Denise and I stood at the cross-roads and that she had chosen the new road and I had chosen the old. This reminds me of the text in Jeremiah 6:16.

Later when my niece was teaching in France, she called on Madame, who asked her to call again the next evening and then she met Denise's two sons, now students in Paris. They took her to see the night-life, places where she could not have gone unaccompanied. So this friendship lasted into the third generation.

When I came to my Cheshire job, I found all the staff friendly and helpful. The senior mistress took me out in her car and showed me where to find good walks "in the hills" and where there was swimming in a mere. Within two years, first Margaret and then Joan had joined the staff and we had many happy outings together. They moved on to more senior posts in girls' schools but we continued to meet at each others' homes. At this period single teachers often spent much of the holidays at home with their parents. So we got to know each others' parents too. In later years, we took many holidays together, mostly in Greece but occasionally elsewhere. Even though those holidays are now past we keep in touch and as far as I know we are all surviving quite well for our ages.

I am glad to be able to record that Margaret and I knew Greece before it was geared to tourism, but we realise that the people have to make a living from the resources they have.

I first met my French friend Madeleine in Yugoslavia. We kept in touch and exchanged visits for many years. She was a Doctor of Pharmacy and from time to time moved from one hospital and /or university to another. When in Algiers she invited me to spend my Easter holidays with her. I arrived late on Thursday evening and was told that she and her cousin, Paul, were taking me down to the desert, starting very early the next morning and this we did, crossing a very fertile belt of land smelling strongly of orange blossom. By mid-day we reached the home of some of Madeleine's former students and I found we were invited to a circumcision feast, in honour of a seven year old boy who had not been "done" at the proper time. He was not enjoying the day! Meanwhile we joined family and friends at a lavish lunch which included whole roast lambs served on copper trays. We tore off pieces of meat by hand, I wished I had known more about Moslem table manners!

After visiting the lad in whose honour the feast was held and being shown his wound, we were taken to a "holy" site, where we saw a mosque and the empty cells of students training for leadership, who were now on vacation. More interesting was an ancient tree which had a legend similar to the Glastonbury thorn.

We stayed the night and then crossed the Atlas Mountains. By evening we reached a town on the edge of the desert. Here we found that, because of some festival, both hotels were fully booked. So what to do? Madeleine recollected a former student who lived nearby and suggested that we call on her. This we did. We sat in a large room, while Madeleine chatted with some of the family and about an hour later she casually let drop that we had nowhere to spend the night. Immediately the whole atmosphere changed and we became welcome guests. From the car we collected what we needed and this included warm coats as blankets might be scarce. Meanwhile in the house preparations were being made to give us real Moslem hospitality. Hot water was brought for hand washing and soon afterwards an ample supply of stewed meat and vegetables arrived and we were left to eat in peace.... then gradually the room filled up, folk of all ages, folk who had come to see the visitors. To my horror I found we were each expected to do something to amuse the company! I decided on something I suppose most English children know, "Here's the church, here's the steeple...."etc, church and steeple became mosque and minaret. I can't imagine what became of this by the time my French had been translated into Arabic by a teenage girl. It was not a great success, but it sufficed!

The next day into the desert and south to the oasis

where we were to stay for the next few days. Everyone knows about oases, but one thing must be recounted. The town was walled and outside there was some scrubby herbage, where sheep and goats were seeking sustenance. The shepherd who was with them wore a long white robe. At nightfall a gate in the wall was opened and the animals, which had been waiting to hear the lift of the latch, raced towards and through the gateway. The shepherd followed carrying a new-born lamb in his arms. I felt I had been transported back to Biblical times! The gate opened on to a track which ran parallel to the wall. Every house had a room entered by a downward slope or it had a shed outside. Inside each was a manger containing food and each animal knew its own home and dashed in eagerly in expectation of a solid meal!

The moonlight that followed was magnificent. It was easy to read by it.

The long journey back to Algiers was done in one day. For a long period of time we were able to see the south side of the Atlas mountains, bathed in sunlight and made up of large areas of brilliantly coloured spring flowers. Even Swiss flowers could not have made a better show!

We arrived "home" very late. I saw crocks on the table and said to myself, "Madeleine has had her help, Fatima, come in to lay the table", but no! what I saw had been left from breakfast a week earlier!

Algeria had been "liberated" by France about a year before I went there, but my bank had not been able to obtain any Algerian currency and I was without money for several days... Madeleine's salary was still paid from Paris.

The next time I visited her, I thought I was going to Nice, but actually spent most of the time in a remote bungalow built at the top of a large area of ancient terracing and with a magnificent view across a village whose name I never managed to learn.

Of course I couldn't give Madeleine holidays to equal those she gave me, but she said she loved Worcestershire because the pastoral scene reminded her of the Normandy she had known in her youth.

Alas! I have recently had news of Madeleine's death.

6.

A STRANGER WITHIN THY GATES

Time passed. The war was over and by 1949 I was a well established member of the school staff, in fact, part of a team who had served throughout the war years and was referred to by the Head as "The Hard Core"! The Head was very internationally minded and most co-operative when I told him I would like to have a fifteen-year-old German girl to stay for six months, but this would only be possible if she could attend school.

Ella's niece was too shy to accept the invitation, but the family knew of another girl who longed for such an opportunity. So Ursula was invited.

Meanwhile the Head had arranged with the

County Education Committee that she should be treated as if she were English, i.e. availability of school dinners, loan of text books, free stationery, and my parents agreed that whenever I came home for half-terms and holidays, she would come with me.

The Head decided that she should go into an A form of her own age group and there she would sink or swim. This was not a form I taught. They were a splendid group of girls and I prepared them for her arrival.

At last the great day came. My sister Joyce was working in London and had time off to meet Ursula at Heathrow, keep her overnight and see her on to the Crewe train in the morning. I had a morning off school to meet her at the station. Only one young person got off the train and she was carrying only a small overnight case. She handed me a letter from Joyce, telling me that Ursula's case had not arrived and that she would see to it and send it on as soon as possible. We then went to the food office to get ration cards. Ursula was very tall and looked older than her age and we were told she must have a work permit to get ration cards. After a tussle, her passport proved she did not need a work permit and we got her ration book. So back to my flat where I gave her a meal and, as we ate, we smiled at each other across the table and I knew it was going to be all right.

I left her writing a letter home and playing with the radio to see what German stations she could get and I went to school and taught my afternoon lessons. (At this point in the story, any experienced teacher laughs!)

The next morning Ursula became a Grammar School pupil and was received on arrival by a welcoming group of her new classmates. From then on I had no need to think about how she would cope with school life.

But the saga of the suitcase was only just beginning! Every evening Joyce got in touch with Heathrow and began sending me postcards saying the case could not be found, eventually a card came claiming that all the airports in Europe had been searched and now they were starting on America! (There were less airports then than now!) However the next card that came said the case had been found at Frankfurt, the point of embarkation and was now at Heathrow, but customs would not release it unopened and the key was in Cheshire...key posted, case examined, Joyce in possession of case...but by this time there was a baggage handlers' strike at Euston. So by telegram I asked Joyce to send it from Paddington via Shrewsbury and so the case arrived and I left Ursula unpacking, while I went to a meeting. All was well except that among her clothes was about half a pint of dry sand!

Looking back at this period, when I had no phone, I realise how efficient the Post Office was.

I had expected to have to supplement the clothes Ursula brought with her and had hoarded some coupons for that purpose. About half way through the three weeks of caselessness, I asked what she missed most and was amazed when she wrung her hands and said, "My Beethoven Sonatas". This lack was soon rectified for the very next day, the music master was able to lend her a set and then she practised every day after school.

This loan of music was only one sign of kindness. As other folk became aware of her, she received many gifts and loans: half a crown a week pocket money, writing paper and stamps, a warm dressing gown, the loan of a bicycle and a gift of a good second hand coat, which fitted well and had only to be dyed navy blue to be school uniform. So now with the purchase of a school beret and tie (no coupons needed), she really began to look and feel like a member of the school.

I remember telling Ursula that she would find all the staff kind and helpful, except perhaps her maths master whose son had been killed in the war. Some weeks later I asked how she got on with him and was told, "It was all right as soon as he found I could do maths." The geography master prepared a special course on Cheshire for her and, after Christmas at my home, a course on Worcestershire.

She had, I knew, to be kept fully occupied and that was no problem. She wrote lengthy letters to Germany. She knitted by the acre (or should I say hectare?) and was soon taking orders for cardigans and jumpers and, though holding the needles in the German way, could follow most English patterns, except lacey ones which defeated us completely. School friends living in the town invited her to tea and sometimes they came to us.

Fortunately, from my point of view, Ursula was a Protestant and came with me to the Baptist Chapel, where she was soon singing in the choir. There was a weekend in the spring term, when we missed the morning service, as we had cycled out to a youth hostel for Saturday night and had taken another girl with us.

And all the time I was teaching a full time-table, preparing lessons, marking books and I do not think any of this was neglected. Do you wonder I had no time to improve my German? But it was good for Ursula's English.

At the end of term Ursula enjoyed the carol concert in the school hall, carol service in the wonderful old parish church and the senior dance. Then she came home with me to a medieval farm-house, no electricity and no mains water. Having lived in Frankfurt throughout the war, she took these deficiencies in her stride. Over Christmas she admitted to one disappointment. She had expected that brandy would be poured over the Christmas pudding and set alight and that flames would leap to the ceiling. She found it difficult to believe that none of us and none of our friends had ever seen such a thing!

Spring term came and went without incident, but on the first day of the Easter holidays we journeyed by train to Torquay. In wartime one of my friends had been evacuated there with her job and she was still there. She invited us to stay for a few days, as, though Ursula had flown over the Channel she had not seen the sea, as it had been cloudy. We had glorious weather and saw Devon at its best. We then had a few days at my home and Ursula joined in "The Long Meadow Picnic" and I think it was the last we ever had. It was a special one because, not only had we a German visitor, but Joyce's fiancé was there and so was a younger generation of Jacksons. Then it was back to school for a few weeks, in which the geography master gave Ursula her own special course on south west England.

Mid-May came and Ursula was now sixteen and due to go home. Joyce again helped her from Euston to Heathrow. This time there were no difficulties with the suitcase but she had acquired so many clothes and goods and chattels that there was a charge for excess luggage. Her form-mates had given her a copy of "Three Men on the Bummel".

For a few days it seemed as if the whole school had gone into mourning!

Ursula and I exchanged Christmas letters for many years and long after her visit she once wrote that she looked back on her time in England as, "Six months in Fairyland". Then there was silence. What happened?

Some years after Ursula went home, a letter

addressed to her arrived at my address. I took the liberty of opening it and found she was being transferred from one doctor's list to another! So I had remembered to get her on to a doctor's list, but quite forgotten to take her off it when she went home.

Later in life, when I had retired and my parents had departed from this world, I lived alone in the bungalow they had built for their retirement. At a Women's Institute meeting, we were asked if anyone would offer to give a deprived child a country holiday in the summer. Well, why not! I volunteered, not for one child but for two, stipulating that they must be sisters or school friends who could share a twin-bedded room. My conditions were gladly accepted and I was told nothing more except their names, ages and where and when to meet the coach bringing them from Coventry.

I knew I had to keep them occupied and gave much thought about how to prepare. Well – scrap books, lots of coloured pictures, paper cutting scissors, cold water paste, brushes, library books for their age group (as recommended by the County Librarian), jig-saw puzzle and clock golf on the lawn.

The great day came and I met the coach in Evesham. I was in for a series of shocks. (1) Two girls much smaller than the height I expected for their eleven and twelve years got off the coach. (2) The lady in charge handed me a paper saying the younger one was epileptic but would be all right if she took her tablets. As we walked down High Street to where I had parked, I suggested we bought a postcard and sent it to their mother to say they had arrived safely. Shock (3) "You'll have to write it, we can't read and write!..." Then there was the question of what they should call me. I had thought of Jackie, but one of them used her second name abbreviated to Jackie. So I asked them to guess what my name was and, after some discussion, they decided it was Sandra. So for the duration of their visit I became Sandra! It was not long before they were known, in the immediate vicinity, as "the Coventry Kids."

Immediately, they made themselves completely at home, making themselves cups of tea whenever they felt like it and looking through all my books to see if there were any with pictures. They were very quick, very agile, very capable and very cheerful. Nothing daunted them. A friend, who was a factory manager, said that they would make excellent workers.

Once again I found friends and neighbours glad to be helpful. The herdsman let them watch him hand-milk the cows every afternoon when we were at home. A lady who was temporarily living in a caravan invited us to tea. Another day they were asked to "tidy" a dolls' house and this gave them plenty of time to play with it. We went to Worcester and took a boat trip on the river… but what I think they found most satisfying was to whirl their arms while racing till exhausted across an open field. Surely young people need space.

Here I must digress. Some years later a women's meeting run by two neighbouring churches was linked with a similar meeting of a Birmingham church. One year for their summer outing, they came to one of our churches for morning coffee, then spent a few hours in Evesham before returning to the other for tea. During a slight lull in conversation, a voice was heard to say, "I don't like it here." Asked why not, the answer came, "Too much space."

The next year I took another pair of "Coventry Kids." They were a year younger than the previous ones, but much bigger and slower. Everything was new to them and whatever I said or did, one of them asked "Why?" and I learnt what parents so often suffer. These girls also needed space, for although there was a garden behind their house, their father had filled it with an aviary and there was nowhere for them to play but the street.

The last pair of sisters who came to me were older, fourteen and fifteen. They had been brought up by foster parents since before they could remember, but had kept in touch with their father. They were well-mannered, well-spoken and one was working on a school project and was helped by our visit to Hartlebury Museum. In each of the three cases, I found out easily without any probing how they came to be 'deprived.' Suffice to say there were no money problems.

One thing about these holidays pleased me greatly. Shortly before they went home, one of each pair said, "And we never turned on the telly once!"

I too have been a stranger within someone else's gates! In 1937, I arranged to spend a week with a pen-friend in South Germany followed by a week's tramping in Belgium and Luxemburg. In between I would have a night in the Cologne Youth Hostel and this was booked in advance. One always hears of the efficiency of the Germans, but the train was two hours late arriving in Cologne and I didn't think I had time to reach the hostel before it closed at 10pm. The train might be late but I had no faith that the hostel Hausvater would let me in if I arrived a minute after 10pm. and the hostel was somewhere right over on the East side of the city.

I sought accommodation in a hotel and at one or two places near the station, but no-one was prepared to take me in. So I wandered down one or two side streets and eventually saw two respectable looking ladies coming towards me. I dared to stop them and explain my predicament and, after some consultation together, they suggested that I should go a little further on and knock on the door of a house whose number they gave me. In faith I did this and the door was opened by an elderly lady, who called her sister and they agreed to put me up for the night. I heard them discussing that, being English, the Fräulein wouldn't mind sleeping on the ground floor. I had my Y.H.A. sleeping bag and they put a cushion and a rug on a settee in the hall. They invited me to eat with them and we ate bread, cheese and salad and, instead of plates, used the little rectangular boards which I knew existed and in former times had been in constant use. Supper over, they explained they were not allowed to keep a foreigner over night unless registered with the police. This was Nazi Germany. So while one of them washed up, the other walked with me, plus passport, to the police station, where I was approved as fit to spend a night in the city. Little did the police know that I was carrying a letter from nuns in a German convent to the nuns in England, who had arranged my pen-friendship and exchange. I had been told that on no account must this letter fall into the hands of German officials, but of course the letter was not with me at the police station.

I cannot remember anything about the next morning. I hope I thanked the ladies, offered payment and wrote when I got home. I caught my train to Brussels, but had a nasty moment as we approached the frontier as a Nazi official came to see what we were carrying out of Germany. The dangerous letter was packed among the dirty clothes I had worn in the first week of my holiday and was now in a cardboard dress box. I was asked what was in the box and feared it would be opened. I could not remember the word for 'dirty' but a German with whom I had been chatting acted as interpreter. The official did just glance inside the box but no more. All was well but I hope not to go through another such experience, for the survival of a whole convent of nuns depended on the fate of that letter.

Within a few years, British bombs had flattened the part of Cologne that had sheltered me.

7.

SHIPS THAT PASS IN THE NIGHT

There are some situations and contacts that last only a few minutes or a few weeks and yet are remembered for a lifetime. Perhaps some of mine are worth recording.

During the First World War there was no conscription of women, but they were invited to give of their time to help at Aldershot. Our governess, Cockie, answered the appeal and worked in the Officers' Mess. There she struck up a friendship with Mr. Strong who, when next on leave, came to stay with her parents and she was invited to bring him to lunch (then called dinner) at Thorn. I think he was a Captain, his uniform immaculate, every button polished and gleaming in the sunshine that poured into the room. He was offered bread to eat with his meal, he took a slice and crumbled it up but scarcely ate any. My mother ticked him off properly, telling him that civilians didn't waste food in wartime. It was the first time I had ever heard a grown-up ticked off. I never saw or heard of him again.

Would it be out of place to recount the only dream that I remember clearly? The sun was shining and I was playing alone in my grandfather's garden. In the middle of the lawn stood a large wooden box and I had been told not to touch it. I thought I would just peep inside, so lifted the lid a tiny bit but it flew open and I found it was a Jack-in-the-box. Up jumped the Kaiser in full uniform to the waist and below the waist just a big spring, not attached to the floor of the box, but allowing him to jump after me as I ran out of the garden into the village street and on....In next to no time I had gone six or so miles, with the Kaiser still behind me as I ran round a quarry I knew. One of the paths crossed a well which was roughly hewn in the rock and I had often been warned about it, so I jumped over the well and the Kaiser jumped into it and I woke up!

I ask myself if this dream was in colour, but can only say that I think the Kaiser's uniform was khaki... but then I had never heard of field-grey!

It was harvest time in 1919 and the weather was glorious. My mother's cousin Honor and her fiancé Viv came to stay. He was an Australian, tall and very strong and still in khaki. Coming from a farm in New South Wales, he understood harvest and every day pitched sheaves faster than anyone had seen before.

In the evenings we all gathered round the piano and Honor accompanied our singing. Viv sang "A Quaint Little House in a Quaint Little Town," which was a great favourite. Dad's repertoire consisted of "The Lincolnshire Poacher," "The Three Crows," "The Little Powder Monkey" and "The Old Soldier" and we all joined in songs from The Scottish Students' Song Book. The visitors had brought with them sheet music of popular songs and, of everything sung, my favourite was "K-K-K-Katie."

Viv's strength became legendary and in following harvests the workers used to mutter, "Wish we had that Australian chap here ! "

Some years have passed and the scene has changed. After morning break a class of pupils sits waiting for a history lesson. The teacher, usually so punctual, is late and then comes in and, before continuing with the syllabus, excitedly tells us what she has been reading in her Daily Telegraph as she drank her cup of coffee. The gist of it was that crop marks had been discovered by aerial photography and this would revolutionise the study of history.

Crewe station is a great place for making short contacts with strangers. There was once a time when I talked to a parrot which was in a cage and the cage stood on an otherwise empty trolley, which stood on an almost empty platform. So I sat on the trolley and talked to the parrot, who really didn't seem very interested. Along strolled a temporarily unemployed porter, who told me the bird had been there since the previous evening and, seeing that it was travelling to a reverend gentleman at a vicarage, staff had organised night shifts trying to teach it bad language, but without any success.

We always broke up several days before Christmas. So how was it that, at 9 a.m. on Christmas Eve, I was waiting on Crewe station for a Birmingham train? This was wartime and every year the Post Office recruited people willing to help with the Christmas rush and most of the candidates were my pupils, but for some years I worked there too. I was given an indoor job while they collected from letter boxes and delivered in the town. I was faced with a huge pile of letters on a large table with vertical sides perhaps six inches high. Postmen, coming in after collecting from boxes, emptied more and more letters on to my tray. My job was to 'face up', i.e. arrange all with stamps at top right hand corners and stack them on edge against the side of the tray. Before that was finished another bag of mail had been dumped in front of me. Whenever I caught up and had a clear tray, I sorted letters into 'locals' and 'forwards'. Occasionally, if I had spare time, I was promoted to sorting parcels into bags addressed to far away places. I wonder how many mistakes I made! I record all this because nowadays, since we have phosphor bands on stamps, and postcodes, much of this work is done electronically. It was interesting to work on equal terms with some of my pupils and to see what scallywags some of them were!

So I travelled home on Christmas Eve. A few

yards along the platform stood a handsome young sailor. He said "Hello"and I glanced in his direction but did not recognise him. After a short pause, he said, "Alcester Grammar School," so I looked again with more interest. Then he added, "Jackson, but I don't know which one." So we travelled together and he told me that after leaving school he had got a degree in German and now had been given four days leave to learn Dutch and then was being posted as interpreter on a ship with an English captain and Dutch crew. His small case was heavy with the necessary books.

Later I heard his ship had gone down 'with all hands'.

Soon after the Second World War ended, part of the Polish Air Force was stationed nearby and a friend asked if I would give English lessons to one of the officers. I agreed readily. When the appointed time came, I was recovering from a bad cold but decided it could no longer be infectious so made no effort to postpone the lesson. So Pisarewski arrived and we read from Youth by Conrad and chatted. He was a very well-educated man and his knowledge of English grammar was probably better than mine. All that he needed was practice in conversation. In the course of the next few meetings he told me something of his life. He had been a lawyer in Warsaw until the Luftwaffe devastated the city and he lost his wife and house and the firm for which he worked. So he joined the Air Force and for a time was stationed somewhere in the Middle East. There he met and married the widow of a former friend who had also lost everything in the Blitz. She too had joined the Forces and soon was able to join him in England.

After the first lesson, our mutual friend asked him how he had got on and was amazed to be told, "Miss Jackson is a little ho(a)rse!"

We exchanged meals and then they soon emigrated to Australia. I never heard from him again, but how could I forget the compliment he paid my cooking, for he said that the lunch I provided reminded him of a meal he once had in the best hotel in Florence! It was macaroni cheese!

One December afternoon at dusk I was just going back to my flat after a long walk. The entry led in from the narrowest part of the High Street and necessarily the pavement at this point was also narrow. There stood a small woman with some sort of stringed instrument hanging on a cord from her neck. To attract attention she twanged a chord and clearly hoped I would give her money. Remembering for once that I had been taught to give beggars food not cash, I asked her in and we climbed the thirty- eight steps to my second floor flat. She sat by an electric fire while I prepared baked beans on toast and made tea. Alas, the toast was too hard for her teeth. She was a traveller, now with a little boy to care for and they lived in a caravan in Chester, where she had a washing-up job in a hotel…but from time to time found the static life more than she could bear. Now she was just finishing three weeks on the road and was on her way back to Chester. As she picked up her instrument, I asked her to play me a little tune and received the reply, "Oh! I can't play!" So I gave her the bus fare to Chester and sent her on her way.

My friend Margaret and I first went to Greece in the early sixties. That Easter tour was based in Athens but took us as far as Delphi and Delos and to reach the latter involved an overnight stay on Mykonos and sailing on by caique. The sun shone, the sky blue, the sea a deep blue, the wind fresh, the waves high and the caique was of the old type with sails, now superseded by motor boats. It was a wonderful experience but I might not have been so happy had Kwells not been invented!

Our leader not only knew Greek history but was fluent in speaking the modern language and keen to show us Greek customs and encourage us to eat traditional Greek food.

Twelve years later, on our third visit to Greece, we were in Rhodes and even then not many Greeks knew English and our Greek was still of the phrase book variety. One afternoon in a village street we greeted a friendly looking woman who returned our smiles and beckoned us into her house, where she served cups of tea and showed us the family photographs, with all the hospitality for which the Greeks were so famous.

Some years later on Skiathos, I asked where were the village people who used to be seen about the countryside and was told that, as far as possible, they now went into hiding during the tourist season!

Again on Crewe Station and the trains are running late! Before my train was expected another long train drew in. I was standing near the front of this train and an American lady leaned out of a carriage window and looked along the platform. She beckoned me and said she wanted a cup of tea, but the trolley was far away at the other end of the platform and she feared she would not have time to get the tea and be back to her place before the train moved on. So I agreed to go and get one for her. Having obtained it and hurrying back as fast as I could I noticed that the L.M.S. washing up was not as good as it should have been. There was a large smudge of lipstick on the cup. Not wanting my American contact to think badly of English hygiene, I managed to use my not quite clean handkerchief to improve appearances. I reached the lady in plenty of time and she insisted on giving me a tiny hand-embroidered handkerchief and said she always carried a few small gifts when she travelled. From time to time I now do the same.

After retiring, I decided that the dates of holidays should no longer coincide with school holidays so I booked a week in Portugal in February. This gave me lots of contacts not only with folk staying in the same hotel but also with people who lived in Faro.

One afternoon, I decided I must go down to the beach and look at the Atlantic rollers. I was the only person there, so I started building a motte and bailey castle, since I had been studying the subject in an evening class. Behind the beach was a high grass covered bank and hidden behind that some houses. Suddenly a little girl about ten years old came bounding down this bank and joined me. Quickly she built the most splendid castle and peopled it with knights and horses made from dry grass from the bank. We spent a happy afternoon together, passing my phrase book back and forth. I was amazed that we could exchange so much information in this way. At one point I saw a woman looking down at us from the top of the bank – no doubt Mother was seeing if her little girl was all right and she went away satisfied. As the tide receded my young friend ran down to the water's edge and picked up lots of fine shells, some of which I still have and some of those so I am told, had come across the Atlantic from the West Indies! When I began to put on socks and shoes, we both realised my feet were covered with oil, so she ran home for a bottle of spirit and I was soon cleaned! We exchanged Christmas cards till she was quite grown up!

Another afternoon I was walking near the town and stopped to sketch the entrance to a farm, an entrance typical of the district. While I was doing this, two youngish teenage girls came back from school. They had enough English for us to exchange a few words and they took me through the stone archway and there I met their mother in her working clothes. Father had spent the day planting potatoes and was now milking a Friesian cow. The girls soon disappeared and left us two oldies making friends without words! We were both amused by shoes, her working shoes and my walking shoes were very different from the dainty shoes the girls had worn to school! I saw the layout of the farmyard with implements in open sheds, but was sorry not to be invited into the house. Nevertheless a happy interlude!

Who remembers Thomas Cadett? When, soon after the war he gave weekly broadcasts from Paris, I was one of his fans. Never did I guess that we would meet. As a guest at a Boxing Day party at Cookhill Priory, there he was, now retired and finding walking and even standing difficult, sitting in an easy chair by a roaring log fire. Among the many grown-up guests was just one teenage girl, who seemed to have no friends to talk to and who looked completely bored. So I took pity on her. She told me that her home was in Paris and her parents had sent her to England for the whole of her Christmas holidays to improve her English. Just then everyone began to move to the music room to sing English carols and that was the last thing she wanted to do. Now Thomas Cadett had remained sitting by the fire, so I ran and told him the situation and he agreed to amuse the girl, I fetched her and left them gabbling away in French and both looking extremely happy. Alas, I had to leave as I was entertaining in the evening and had a meal to prepare.

In London, I spent a morning at the first day of an art exhibition in honour of Stubbs, but including many other pictures of country scenes, both French and English. I looked at them intently, close up and from a distance. As I seemed to be in the way of a photographer, I apologised and moved, but was told to go back. That evening I was on T.V. but unfortunately did not see the programme – however all this is beside the point.

Towards the end of the morning, I was in conversation with an American lady and we went out to lunch together. She told me of lots of exciting and learned things she did 'back home.' Eventually to keep up my end I told her, quite truthfully, that I was writing a trigonometry text book and she rejoined, "You will have it published in New York as well as London, won't you?" Alas, it was never published. New maths was arriving and my book would have to be abandoned.

The twenty-first century brought a completely new experience. Driving home from a Sunday afternoon service at a tiny Baptist chapel there was very little traffic and I was enjoying the sunshine. Then I thought there was a car following me much too closely. I increased my speed and so did the other car. When I made a quick turn into the side road that led towards home, I was still followed. I should have to stop somewhere and it might as well be outside my house. My pursuer and I stood opposite each other. I heard a soft voice say, "I'm sorry if I frightened you, but did you know you've got a flat tyre?" This was true and I then realised why the side road, which was overdue for resurfacing, had seemed even worse than I expected. Then he added, "Would you like me to change the wheel for you?" It was offered kindly and I accepted gladly.

All's well that ends well !

8.

YUGOSLAVIA

Yugoslavia! What a wonderful name! I first visited it in August 1939. Again I went with I.T.T., this time for strenuous mountain walking (boots essential!) and nights to be passed in mountain huts.

After the long train journey across Europe, we had a meal at an inn and I ate goulash for the first time, very hot, very strong and the best I have ever tasted. We were then welcomed into private houses and I slept in a room with hand-embroidered sheets and curtains. At the foot of the bed stood a locally made chest painted in bright colours of traditional design.

Anyone who has done mountain walking can picture the next ten days but when we came down to civilisation, we found the roads almost empty of motor vehicles and were told that doctors were almost the only people who had cars. We moved from Slovenia into Croatia for two nights, just to see what city life was like in Zagreb and there found much talk of imminent warfare. Searchlights swept the sky while we sat outside a café near the Well of Peace and Mustafa served the coffee with his customary calm.

Late the next evening our leader received a message from the consulate saying that we ought to start our journey home by the night train but, as some of the party were out, this proved impossible. So as planned we caught the 5 a.m. train and there at the station was the consul's secretary, wearing raincoat over pyjamas. He had brought a message saying that when we got to Munich we were to contact the consul to find out if it was safe to take the long journey north and, if not, find an alternative and shorter route out of the country. At Munich we were told we could go on the usual route but must be out of Germany in twenty four hours.

By this time it was getting dark and, as we had

had scarcely a mouthful of food since 4 a.m., we began looking for some and found a refreshment room on the station. Here they could serve dry bread and omelettes and most of us were content with that but, when the meal came, the omelettes had minced ham mixed with the egg… One of our party, who was a Jew, ate only a little dry bread.

So we moved to the platform, where we found the longest train I could possibly imagine. Tourists had all left Germany the previous day and now the residents, with as much of their belongings as they could transport, were leaving. Fortunately we had reserved seats and had no trouble finding them. Platforms were seething with men seeing off wives and families, Germans saying, “Auf Wiedersehen” to English friends. So we set off and the train steamed away.

There were few stops and at each one the platforms were crowded. Years later, Ella told me she had been to Frankfurt station looking for me, but we never saw each other.

There was no singing of the Lorelei on that train. We reached Cologne in the early morning and were glad to find a refreshment room open. Here the menu was ersatz coffee, fresh white rolls and jam. When asked if butter was available, the waiter, a man old enough to remember the First World War, said sadly, "We have guns not butter" and then asked why we had not gone yesterday when all the tourists went.

So we moved on to Brussels where we would surely find solid food! But again we were frustrated, for every establishment that normally sold food and drink was closed.

The Belgian army had been mobilised and the streets were full of men mostly wearing some khaki garments and roaming about looking miserable. We were told that, at the time of the Munich crisis the previous year, the army had been mobilised and the pavements of the capital were littered with drunken men! The authorities were not going to let that happen again.

So, still hoping for sustenance, we moved on to Bruges, where we were able to get afternoon tea…and then on to the coast where the expected boat awaited us. I arrived at Evesham station only ten minutes late and there was Dad waiting for me.

After the war I was able to go to Yugoslavia several more times and I shall write a little about some memorable incidents. Gradually I was learning a few words of Serbo-Croat, but have now forgotten it all!

One very hot day we were tramping in Croatia and came upon a village which had a shop and went in to see what they sold. We were delighted with what we saw and I was able to try out my skill. My side of the conversation went like this:

Good day
Please
Ice cream
Coffee flavour
Thank you
How much? (holding out a handful of coins)
Goodbye.

There was laughter all round! And a tiny spark of international friendship glowed for a moment.

Having only a short distance to tramp, it was decided we should have a free morning. The sun shone brightly and I decided to explore a tempting looking cart track leading into woodland. I passed a cottage and soon came to a clearing containing a vegetable garden, where a woman was picking stick beans. My greeting led to a short conversation in German and then she said she had enough beans and invited me back to the cottage, where I could meet her sister who spoke English. Gladly I went with her and her sister was beside the window and working with a sewing machine. Over coffee I was able to piece together something of their story. They had befriended a G.I. from a unit stationed nearby and the seamstress had expected, not without encouragement, to marry their friend and go out to the U.S.A. when the war was over. She learnt English in preparation for life there… but the Yanks departed and she was left behind. Now the sisters lived together. One looked after the garden and did most of the housework, while the other earned money by dressmaking and upholstery.

Several holidays later, still with I.T.T., we spent a day in Dubrovnik before moving into Bosnia by bus along the almost finished new motor road. There was an hour's break in Mostar, said in winter to be the coldest place in Europe and in summer the hottest. That day it was very hot and I had no desire to walk a short distance to see the famous medieval bridge, which I hear was badly damaged in recent warfare and has now been restored to its former state.

Moving further East we found we were in a land of mosques and minarets, for we were now in a

Moslem world. Then came a long hold-up for, when blasting to widen the still unfinished road, an enormous rock had fallen and completely blocked the road to traffic. Gradually a small queue of vehicles formed on either side. Two women, one of them carrying a tiny baby, got out of an ambulance on the far side, walked past the rock and a car on our side managed to turn and drove away with them.

At last it was decided that the only way to open the road involved further blasting and traffic must reverse for half a kilometre. This was possible for cars but not so easy for a wagon drawn by four bullocks!

No wonder we arrived at Sarajevo somewhat late! At the end of their day's work, people were queuing very tidily for buses, and we joined the appropriate queue, moved forward from time to time and eventually arrived at the Bosnian Alpine Club. After a meal, I looked round for my boots and then realised I must have left them standing in the square where we had queued. The distance was not far, so two of us walked back and found the square completely empty of people, but with my boots standing just where I had left them. What joy! No-one had stolen them, but who would want someone else's well-worn tramping boots and no-one had handed them in at the police station. Imagine the complications there might have been!

Bosnia was by no means lacking in interest. We came upon a Turkish village, where the children knew no other language, did not know what to do with wrapped toffees and were intrigued by a portable radio which always played. As Vlado, its owner said, "to save the English the trouble of singing as they walk through the countryside."

Having so faithfully served a generation, the organisers of I.T.T. were ready to retire. I joined two tramps arranged by well-known commercial companies, but both lacked the high ideals to which I had become accustomed. I too was coming to the end of my tramping days and with a former colleague began a series of holidays in Greece. Later we were joined by a third friend and occasionally by others.

I visited my beloved Yugoslavia once more. In 1964, a friend, who had led one of my early tramps, asked me to go with her to this country which she had never visited. She feared the extreme heat of summer, so we went for a week in my Whitsun half-term and made our own arrangements to travel by air and stay in a hotel in Dubrovnik. Every traveller has a tale to tell about a flight! Here, suffice to say, we landed three times at Zagreb and were given cups of Turkish coffee and had breakfast at Belgrade airport, which was quite off our route. When eventually we set off again, the sun was shining brightly as we circled north of the airport and I am delighted to have seen the wonderfully fertile agricultural plain that stretches so far across central Europe.

We took a day trip to Montenegro. There were not many people on the coach and we had good views all around it. We came to a long stretch of straight road. On the right was a steepish hillside thickly covered with trees and bushes, on the left the land was fairly flat. One other vehicle came towards us from the furthest point we could see.... as we moved forward we saw a bundle in the middle of the road. Both vehicles stopped as they approached it and the drivers got out and talked together. The car driver picked up the bundle carefully, put it in his car and continued on his journey. Our driver spoke good English and explained what we had seen. Thereabouts were many Romany families, who wanted some or all of their children to be able to become part of the modern world, so a baby might be wrapped in a rug and left in the middle of the road, while the mother hid among the bushes and watched. If the bundle was picked up she knew the child would be brought up in a modern orphanage, if not picked up she took it home and tried again another day.

Is it really more than a quarter of a century since I last visited my beloved Yugoslavia? In those years it has suffered much and it still suffers.

9.

RETIREMENT

'Shorter in wind, as in memory long'
Harrow Football Song.

I asked myself, where do I go from here? For some years I had not been able to travel far from home, so in the first year I visited my French friend in May and my German friend in autumn and at home devoted myself to my quarter acre garden....but there's more to life than that.

Long ago I had decided that it was a good thing I had done badly in my Higher School Certificate. Had I passed with distinction, my whole life would have been different. I would have stayed on for a third year in the sixth form trying for scholarships, which I now know I would not have obtained, thus wasting a year. So I was at Reading in the Lent term of 1931 and attended a Christian mission where I made the greatest decision of my life and I was baptised by total immersion the following autumn. I tried to serve God in my daily work and witnessed by chapel attendance on Sundays. Now, having retired, I had no work in the ordinary sense, so devoted time and energy helping at the chapel I had known since childhood. Times were changing and many congregations of small chapels in tiny hamlets were in difficulties. Young people moved away and the cottages were bought by newcomers, new houses were built. Folk who wanted Sunday services could get in their cars and travel to bigger and more lively places of worship.

I started in a simple way, clipping with sheep shears round the headstones in the graveyard, but was soon on a flower and cleaning rota, was a member of the women's meeting and then its secretary. In due course I became deacon and treasurer, with only one other active person to do all the duties. The flower and cleaning rota had sunk to one! Eventually the church had to be closed and I moved to one of its daughter churches.

Of course I had time and energy for other pursuits and soon after retirement I teamed up with a retired farmer whose family had lived in the parish for generations and who had always taken a lively interest in what was going on around them. They had kept diaries, which were passed on to younger generations. These my new friend summarised, while I made countless visits to the Record Office. I had splendid help from the staff there and went through everything I could find about the parish, but was defeated by the handwriting and English in the earliest wills. In due course we published four books of parish history but, in later years, we found mistakes, particularly in the archaeology. However I found trained archaeologists very kind and was told they were very happy to have other people's ideas brought to their attention, so that they could be proved or disproved.

I once heard my co-author asked how we managed to write together and his reply was, "I write what I like and she does what she likes with it."

Not long after the fourth book was published my friend died and I was thankful we had taken our writing as far as we could go.

Local history having ceased to occupy my time, I

needed a new ploy. By now, the friend with whom I first went to Greece, was free from family responsibilities and we went abroad together every year, mostly to Greece of which the ancient history and legends had fascinated her since college days at Oxford. So I decided to take up Linguaphone Greek, which proved very interesting and time-consuming. I got far enough to feel I could cope with 'island hopping,' but my friend is more timid than I and would have none of it. So we continued as 'tourists'. We visited many ancient and beautiful sites situated on mainland and islands and gradually, as we got older and less able to climb hills, sought sea and sun. In later years we were joined by a friend with whom we had worked in wartime and who kindly took over the making of all arrangements.

In Greece there are many things I would like to have seen and done. I have vivid memories of a Greek Easter in Rhodes and I would love to visit Philippi again. I did not even manage to buy a picture postcard of the meadow where Paul met Lydia and other women or of the nearby river where baptisms took place. We were shown the prison where Paul and Silas were said to have been incarcerated but know other tourists have been shown a different one and nearby there are several possibilities. A day trip to Ephesus was much too short, as was our time in Corinth and I would like a few more days on Samos to check upon a discovery I think I made there. If I was right, no doubt the inhabitants already know all about it! A visit to Patmos is unforgettable. For a few minutes my friend and I were alone in the cave where St. John is believed to have lived and written the Book of Revelation while he was in exile. Then other tourists poured into the cave and the atmosphere was lost.

Eventually the time came to give up all thoughts of further holiday's abroad and I needed a new interest. Those who have read my story thus far know what I decided to do!

As my strength deteriorates, so does my garden, though I am glad to have some help from a kind neighbour. It is no longer a riot of flowers, but a wilderness of weeds, interspersed with a few hardy perennials. However, I find young people seem to like it this way!

As I sit in comfort and view the Boat Race, I recall the first year I took any interest in this event. Family loyalties were divided and I backed Cambridge. In those days we did not know the result instantly as we do today, but had to wait for the newspaper to be delivered on Monday morning. While we were still at breakfast, I was tantalised by Dad saying, "The Light Blues won," for I was too young to know that teams were distinguished by the colours they wore. I was kept guessing for some time!

Later in that year I heard of agricultural shows and my mind goes back to the time when such shows were resumed after World War 1 and Oliver was taken to one. I was very jealous! He came home and talked a lot about tents, which had made a great impression on him. The next day Dad brought together four wooden sheep hurdles, made two inverted V's tied firmly together with binder twine and then carefully arranged a wagon sheet over them. So for the rest of the summer we had our own tent on a bit of land still known in the family as 'The Show Ground'.

On Christmas Eve as I sit alone listening to carols from King's College my mind strays back to those wonderful Christmases we had at Grandpa J's home in Reading. The programme went something like this – stockings – everyone to chapel in the morning – Christmas dinner, sometimes for as many as twenty four (Dad carved an enormous turkey for, being a farmer, he was supposed to understand the anatomy of a bird better than anyone else present) – Christmas pudding or fruit salad and everyone got a sixpence – dessert in the drawing room – up to the billiard room to admire a splendidly decorated tree and watch from a window for Father Christmas in full regalia as he came out of a wood where he had left his reindeer, amazing how an uncle was always absent – wonderful presents! – tea for those who needed reviving – Victorian party games, but as the average age of grandchildren increased, other forms of entertainment were introduced – once a Punch & Judy Show, once a conjuror and once a whist-drive!

It must have been after the war that a Boxing Day programme emerged. In the morning a small charabanc drew up at the gate and those who wished climbed in and were taken to a meet of the hounds outside a village pub. Everything from the stirrup cup to the mummer's performance was done in the time-honoured way. When the hunt moved off to draw a nearby coppice we started for "home". In the afternoon, uncles went to football, and aunts and cousins to the pantomime.

We did not go to Reading every year for sometimes Dad felt he should stay on the farm and work there, so that the stockmen could have a real holiday.

My latest interest is the discovery that my little home stands on the site of a Romano-British farm!

While writing these pages my memory has roamed over nearly ninety years and now I feel that I am becoming a female version of

"… the lean and slippered pantaloon
with spectacles on nose."

Time marches on and, if I be spared, I soon shall reach the stages of

"… second childishness, and mere oblivion,
Sans teeth, sans eyes, sans taste,
sans everything."

As You Like It. Act II Scene vii

But all is not lost. I am thankful to find I have so many friends and neighbours with hearts of gold.

* * *